NO WORD OF LOVE

No Word of Love

A. L. BARKER

CHATTO & WINDUS
THE HOGARTH PRESS
LONDON

Published in 1985 by
Chatto & Windus · The Hogarth Press
40 William IV Street
London WC2N 4DF

British Library Cataloguing in Publication Data

Barker, A. L.
No word of love.
I. Title
823′.914[F]   PR6003.A678

ISBN 0 7011 2900 X

F 5,5 2 7

£9.50

Photoset in Linotron Ehrhardt by
Rowland Phototypesetting Ltd
Bury St Edmunds, Suffolk
Printed in Great Britain by
Redwood Burn Ltd
Trowbridge
Wiltshire

To Paul Sheridan

Three of these stories have been published previously: 'Eve' appeared in the anthology, *You Can't Keep Out the Darkness* (Bodley Head 1980); 'An Excellent Thing in a Woman' appeared in *Nova* magazine (1973) and in P.E.N.'s *Broadsheet* (1984); 'A Communications Failure' appeared in *Fiction Magazine* (1982).

CONTENTS

EVE   1

THE TWICHILD   14

AN EXCELLENT THING IN A WOMAN   33

BELLE-AMIE   48

NO WORD OF LOVE   88

HIS WONDERS TO PERFORM   98

A COMMUNICATIONS FAILURE   106

ROOM FOR ONE LESS   116

BISCUIT   134

WOUNDS INCURRED IN THE MATING SEASON   155

THE DAY'S RAGE, THE NIGHT'S REGRET   168

EVE

When Mel Towne went to Flinder's Farm he was making an unsteady living modelling for knitting leaflets and true-story magazines: evenings and weekends he worked at his painting, which made nothing. He had mobile good looks which could be reorientated by a hair-parting. With earburns and a divide down the middle he was quite the devil, but bring the comb across to one temple and he became a clean-limbed fellow. Give him a quiff and he was every mother's son. As a model he was much in demand; if anything, he was over-exposed.

Those were the days, the 1930s, when young men parted their hair. There was no other special virtue in the period, but it is feasible – more feasible anyway – to suppose that there were still people in existence then who combined social ignorance and primeval know-how. It would be fairly incredible nowadays. Young people on outlying farms – if there are any young people on outlying farms – are so much more forward. When everything is a marketable commodity, and they even see their sex changing hands all the time, who would have the gall, let alone the naivety, to try to tell them that miracles only happen once?

Mel was twenty-six, he hadn't been trained, he had taught himself to paint and with his talent and potential he considered that he had an inalienable right to be doing nothing else. If he didn't come to be uttered in the same breath as old Leonardo, he confidently expected to outclass the middleweights like Picasso and Palmer.

He came across the farm one Saturday afternoon when he was walking the downs from Salisbury, looking for something to sketch. There were plenty of subjects but he was not in the mood to immortalise any old ivied cottage or ferny dell. The day had been without inspiration and when he was kicking his way through the nettles that

[1]

grew along the farmyard wall and saw Mrs Flinder throwing tea-leaves into the midden he realised that he needed refreshment.

She brewed him a pot of tea and served, unasked, a slab of seedcake with it. She accepted the shilling he offered in payment and he opened the kitchen door to leave. But seeing the Wiltshire downs, miles and miles of them, in decolorant cloud, he asked if he could stay the night. He felt provoked into trying to get the sheer inertia of the hills on to his drawing-board.

Next morning Mrs Flinder brought him eggs, bacon, tomatoes and fried bread. 'Five shillings?' he said, keeping his finger on the plate – 'For supper, bed and breakfast?' She nodded and he started on the bacon. It was good, rich and pungent, and he told her so.

'We killed the pig at Michaelmas.' She jerked her thumb. 'She did the dying.'

Mel looked behind him. A girl stood beside the dresser, her head did not reach the first row of plates. He nodded, he didn't like children, and went on with his breakfast. When she came to clear away he could see that she might be any age between twelve and twenty. She had lint-white hair and skin the colour of low-grade milk. He judged her to have been seriously deprived of something.

'What's your name?'

'Flinder.'

'Polly?'

She held his greasy plate to her chest, rinds and all, and she did not smile.

'Her name's Eve,' said the mother. 'We always said if we got a boy we'd call him Adam.'

Mel went out and sketched the farm. It was a nice thing to draw: there was challenge in its sturdy appropriation of the picturesque, like the old Boule Neige roses over the porch and the dead crow nailed spread-winged to the barn door.

The girl watched from a distance until Mrs Flinder came and called her. 'Evvy, have you fed the hens? Sweep this floor, shake these mats. What are you gawping at?'

[2]

Did she know? he wondered, busily cross-hatching under the eaves. An hour later the sketch was finished. He stood looking at it, flexing his fingers as was his habit when pleased. He was thinking that it would make a little study in oils that should stand comparison with Van Gogh's 'Chaumière'.

Out of the corner of his eye he saw the girl still watching and he beckoned to her. She moved slowly, as if she were coming through deep water. 'There it is,' he said. 'Flinder's Farm for posterity.' Her ponderous gait could be due to the difficulty of keeping her feet inside a pair of shoes that were sizes too big for her. She gazed at his sketch, frowning, and earnestly, he saw, trying for something. He thought it must be understanding, for obviously she would have trouble correlating brain and eye. 'What do you make of it?'

'Why is it black?'

'It's charcoal, that's why.'

'Our house is white.'

'You have to draw white with black. Like clean and dirty, you don't know you're clean till you've been dirty.'

He started another drawing and forgot her. It was a not altogether pleasurable surprise when he stopped again, later, and saw her still there, waiting to accomplish that simple feat of understanding. He put his hands on his knees and, stooping, looked into her eyes.

He had always thought that grey eyes signified a calculating nature. Hers were a dark, troublous pearl, set in white lashes that neither introduced nor defined them – one went straight from skimmed milk into the depths of the sea. It wasn't logical and it wasn't art.

Moved to repair the deficiency, he took her by the chin. She did not resist while he blacked her brows and ringed her eyes with charcoal. 'There,' he said, 'that's better.'

It wasn't. She looked grotesque. He had to laugh. Nature was right, he thought, and picked up the corner of her pinafore. 'Go and wet this in the trough and clean your face.'

He went back to the farm the following weekend, made a habit of going there throughout the spring and summer. The accommodation was cheap, the food good and there was something he wanted to say about the place. He brought his oils and an old easel which he stowed in the barn when he left, and he sketched and painted the farm from every angle. From the top of Fossbury Beacon it looked like a black and white cat curled up in an armchair.

When it rained he sketched in the kitchen – Mrs Flinder as she went about her cooking, or Flinder himself as he sat to eat. Not the girl: rain or shine, he felt no wish to draw her.

Once he tried a caricature of her as a stick-insect. She had a knack of merging with the background. He did not always see her, yet he always felt when she was there. She bugged him rather, standing and staring. Wherever he looked for her, high or low, he always seemed to look right into her eyes, which was a pointless exercise. They went through into her head without reservation or ambiguity, she had no need of either, because God alone knew what went on in her mind.

'Is she all right?' he said cheerfully tapping his forehead as they all sat at dinner one day. She was gazing raptly at him across the table and did not turn a hair. Mrs Flinder tightened her mouth like a purse and Flinder, a preternaturally silent man, threw his knife across his plate. Mel said quickly, 'Is she going to be all right, I mean? What will she do when she leaves home? What sort of job?'

'She ain't be leaving.'

'But you can't keep her here for ever. You can't rely on *your* being here for ever.'

'She'll marry and have her own place. We can see to that.'

Mel couldn't. He tried, as he ate Mrs Flinder's mutton stew, to picture Eve baking and dusting and pegging out shirts. He couldn't. He couldn't see her in the arms of a nice young husband. Or a nice old husband. All he could see was her wading across the yard in her big shoes, watching him with her marine eyes. He meant to ask the girl herself what she wanted to do. If she had no ideas of her own it might be a kindness to give her some. In fact – the laugh, that time, was on him – he gave her just the one . . .

It was a Saturday afternoon, he was painting down by the stream in what was known as the Old Meadow. 'One day,' he said, 'people will come to look at Flinder's, at the house and the barn and the orchard, they'll come and stand where you're standing now –' She always stood, she could be relied on never to make herself easy – 'and they'll talk about it and write about it and there won't be a grain of truth in any of it.' She didn't know what he meant, he was himself trying to figure something out. 'Flinder's I can make what I like of. It's not special, d'you see? It's been here a long time, under the hill, a nice solid little farm, and people have worked it and died and been born in it and it hasn't picked up a single solitary message. Not a peep out of anyone.' He stayed his hand from dashing away at the beautiful cross-patterns of the reeds. She was listening, her eyes on his face, drinking up every word, heard and unheard. It was true, she did have some sort of thirst: suppose it wasn't for knowledge? 'It's mute, I can make it say anything.' He was talking to himself, identifying his motives. He couldn't recall having motives before, the over-riding necessity was to paint and it provided life, reason, faith – all except the etcetera emotions. His scruples were artistic, not moral. But Flinder's was very relative to his work. 'Everything matters, and this place matters a lot. I've got to figure it out, it won't be enough to say "I just felt like it." And I won't have them tying me up with it as they've tied Palmer up with Shoreham.' He saw something, a quickening of the tension in her face, a breath gathered as if she was about to speak. But she opened her mouth and let the breath out. 'The damned biographers will get it all wrong.' He struck a lecturer's pose in front of his easel. ' "We come now to a turning point in the painter's life. From this time forward, whether he was aware of it or not, there was a change of direction, a new and vital factor came into his work –" Of course the painter's aware of it, he's aware of everything,' he flung himself down on the grass, lay on his back with his arms linked under his head – 'even of Eve.' He meant that she should see a little bit of the joke and smile. Then it dawned on him that he never had seen her smile, nor seen any emotion in her face. In her eyes was a beginning, the stuff of something – no knowing how it would turn out.

He sat up to ask her, 'How did you look when they killed the pig?'

She showed him. She was like a very young child devouring its grief. She filled her lungs, she opened her mouth, the tears shot out all over her skin. She was rigid with noise. Mel winced, waiting for the burst, the roar. But she clapped her hands first over her mouth and then her ears. The sounds she had heard, she was plainly hearing again. She sank to her knees and wrapped her arms about her head. Her face, between her elbows, was an O of misery.

'Hey, what a fuss! That's life, that's all – pigs are bacon when they die. Only a booby would cry over it. I took you for a grown-up girl.' Mel, lying in his teeth, smiled encouragingly, and went to her to loosen her arms which were still wrapped round her head. At his touch she fell apart. Like a rag doll, he thought. He was untempted.

Funny how it happened, and funnier that it happened at all. Mel wasn't one to organise that sort of thing: when he had positive inclinations he was prepared to take the necessary steps. It was his experience that women could be swiftly detached from whatever people or principles they felt bound to. Only a small contributory effort was required from him, enough to persuade him he had won the lady and to let her think she had been wooed. He liked a degree of anticipation and he would have said, he would have sworn, that to have the business come out of the blue would be to find him wanting. Or rather, quite unwanting. And coming out of the yellowish afternoon, he and this ageless, well-nigh sexless little creature, it was the oddest and not the loveliest thing ever to happen to him.

He remembered little about it afterwards. No details came to mind, except for one ludicrous moment when she rolled her head aside, blinked her white lashes at him and asked, fearfully, 'Are you going to eat me?'

He sent her away as soon as it was over. She went back to the house and he went on with his work. The obvious, the only course, was to forget that it had happened. He found that easy to do. It was a non-contributory incident, added nothing to his development as an artist. One might say – he did say – that it was a bodily function. He was

[6]

relieved rather than grateful and there was no need to give it another thought.

After supper, the girl had gone to bed and he was able to sit down with the parents with an unclouded conscience. He rather enjoyed their presence, it could hardly be called company. They were solitary people and let him talk. They did not appear to communicate much between themselves by word of mouth. Flinder seldom opened his except to remove or admit his pipe, and Mrs Flinder sat sewing with an ironical expression which Mel respected. For that reason he tended to talk about other people rather than about himself. He had a fund of scandalous stories and it amused him to spill beans – which, spilled elsewhere, might have shot up into big ugly plants – into the quiet of the farm kitchen, between the stately ticking of the clock and the hoot of the owls.

He had been talking about a certain actress when Mrs Flinder said, 'She's latched on to you.'

'Me?' They could scarcely have heard of the woman. 'Why do you say that?'

'She's got her eye on you.'

'Flattering, but unlikely.'

'She ain't only had it on nothing before.'

'Who are you talking about?' His stomach lurched slightly. Mrs Flinder lifted her thumb to the ceiling.

'She's seventeen come Monday.'

'Eve?'

'Young girls is giddy as the volvulous, but she's clean. We seen to that.'

'Clean?' When she was grubby from the fires she had to lay and the potatoes she had to fetch and the beer-coloured mud of the yard?

Flinder took his pipe from his mouth and spoke. 'She never had a grass wedding.'

'A grass wedding?'

'She's never mucked about with boys,' said Mrs Flinder. 'And she's biddable.'

[7]

Mel looked her in the eye. 'What's that to me?'

'You could do worse.' She returned his gaze and then transferred hers to her needle. She threaded it and bit off the cotton and went on with her sewing.

Flinder, who was also threading – wire for his rabbit snares – said, 'Maybe he thinks he could do better.'

Mel yawned elaborately. 'D'you know what I think? I think I'll turn in.'

When he got up to his room he fumed for a while and paced about. Then he dropped on to his bed, and thought. The girl, of course, was the funny side, but before he fell about laughing he should remember that Mrs Ironical Flinder, looking through the eye of her needle, saw him as a prospective son-in-law – whether she knew what had happened that afternoon or not. If she didn't know, she was more than ambitious, she was an unbridled opportunist.

He almost stood up and walked out then and there. But there was the picture he was working on, the view of the brook and the watersplash and the trembling poplars. He wanted to finish it. Tomorrow, he told himself, just the one more day, and then he would go and never come back. He slept that night in his clothes.

Next morning he was able to adjust his fears to a more natural caution. The girl brought his breakfast and cleared away afterwards. He watched her as she took up the crockery with her same near-passion – as if she expected it to jump out of her grasp. It just might, he thought: she was the age and type to conjure up poltergeists. Mrs Flinder asked if he would be staying to dinner.

'Flindergeists.'

'Eh?'

'It depends how soon I finish.'

'Finish?' He could see the short hairs stirring suspiciously.

'My work.'

She nodded. 'I seen you sitting scretting.'

Mel laughed. She was cunning as far as she went, but that, after all, wasn't very far.

He fetched his easel and canvas from his room and went down to the meadow. It was a fine morning: the light, of course, was entirely different. At this hour the splash was in shadow and the water, which had been the focal point, merely lurked. It was now the aspens that glittered and ran in the wind. He was going to enjoy settling the conflict between the water and the trees.

But before he could begin, while he was stroking his nose with a dry brush and watching the poplars racing their leaves, the girl came. This time she did not emerge, she arrived, walking right down his line of vision. Apart from the fact that she was not a graceful mover, it was tiresome to watch. He wanted to get on with his work.

Suddenly he had a gratuitous glimpse of her point of view. He saw that she had a tiny right, a shred of reason. It was beyond her wit, and certainly beyond her experience, to take what had happened as an interlude. He didn't even know what she had made of it. If she asked, whatever she asked, she was entitled to an answer.

'Hallo, Eve. Are you off to church?'

She had on the mucky pinafore which she wore for her jobs about the farm. He didn't want to tease her but he felt a bit awkward seeing her come across the meadow like a dog that had been whistled for – knowing that he had not whistled. He would never put his lips together and blow to bring her.

She said, 'Are you going away?'

'Yes. When I've finished my picture.'

'What will I do?'

'You? Why, what you've always done – feed the hens, have your supper and go to bed.'

'I don't want to.'

He could understand that. She had caught him in an understanding mood. 'You know, I don't think I've ever seen you in your Sunday-go-to-meeting coat. Is it blue or yellow?'

'It's plum.'

'It ought to be apple.' Her eyes reminded him of the yeasty depths under Brighton pier. 'What do you want, Eve?'

'To stay with you.'

'Stay as long as you like.' She would like as long as he stayed, and that, after all, wasn't going to be long.

'I want –' She caught his hand and held it as if it were an independent creature that might fly away – '*that* again,' and she drew his hand to her breast.

'Well I'm damned.'

She came close, folding herself into his hollows.

He tried to laugh. 'You want it now?' He could feel her heart swelling her chest, lifting and actually filling his hand with her small breast. Her lips were parted, her tongue arched, without coquetry or provocation, simply as if she were thirsty.

Her eyes quelled him. In the clouded pearl of each iris were points of flame: they exploded, he would swear they did, like tiny rockets. He had a sense of utter nonentity, annihilation. For an awful ultimate moment he was squeezed out of himself, he was nothing but the mechanics, the means to some all-over-riding, non-risible end.

As he said to himself afterwards, reflecting – though not in tranquillity – sex wasn't in it. Not the boy meets girl sort. It went much, much farther back than that, back to the beginning of life. It *was* the beginning, the first, foremost motive power, inextinguishable, inexorable, and, in her skinny little body, looking out of her eyes, it was bigger than the universe.

He shoved her violently away. Folded against him, she had no balance, she fell. There they were, he with his arm raised to fend her off, she on the ground like a wrecked scarecrow.

'You can't have it. D'you hear?' She did of course hear, his voice was rising with his panic. He was shouting, beside himself, right outside himself – he had a good view of the ridiculous figure he was cutting. 'You can't!'

She flinched and turned away her face. 'You can't!' echoed back from the hill. A leathery bird took off from the poplars with a caw like laughter.

She heard the bird and she shuddered. He saw the cold run over her skin. She pulled herself up on her elbow and looked up at him. 'Why can't I?'

She was then about ten years old, no flame, no afflatus, divine or otherwise, batting her stubby white lashes and opening her mouth, ready to grizzle. A phrase came into his mind – 'the picture of misery'. Not one he would want to paint.

He went down on his heels beside her. 'You can only have it once, d'you see? Once in a lifetime.' He was surprised how quickly she saw, perhaps because she had feared as much. 'It was a miracle and miracles only happen once.' There were a few people he would like to have shared that joke with.

'You mean like God did to the Virgin Mary?'

To his credit, he didn't even smile. He nodded.

She sighed, climbed awkwardly to her feet and set off across the meadow without another glance at him. He watched her go, thinking, as far as he was thinking anything, what a story it would make. Would anyone believe him? Would anyone believe *her*?

Of course it was the finish of Flinder's. He wouldn't be coming again. He didn't need to. The word was 'finish', not 'end', because this picture was going to be the best he had yet done, it was going to be the peak of this period, the final achievement. He could say – his biographer could – that it had happened in the nature as well as the art of things.

He worked through the morning and into the afternoon without stopping. It was marvellous, his hands seeming to minister rather than perform. Rarely and gloriously it could happen like this, the picture waiting on the canvas for him.

No one came, the farm was out of sight and all but his work was out of his mind. Finally, he judged that he had done enough for the picture to be irrefutable. It could be finished anywhere, in Beckenham or Baku. He had caught and fixed the essence of this place. Fifty years on, people looking at his painting would be dropped right here under Fossbury Beacon. He stood before the easel, seeing the quiet, the smell of water, the Sunday bells across the meadows, the leaf which he had crushed between his fingers in order to know the texture of it. He had, and was entitled to, one of those moments of unalloyed happiness such as Leonardo must have experienced.

He cleaned his brushes and wiped his palette, wondering at his gifts. In early youth, offered the choice, he would have opted for the gift of making money. He was glad there had been no choice. Apart from the rage, sweat and joy of the work itself, he would not have wished for other than the artist's life, precarious, various, lonely and free. Here today, gone tomorrow. Correction, he thought, shouldering his easel; here today, gone today.

He crossed the field to the farm gate. Flinder and Mrs Flinder were milking, he could hear them rattling the pails in the cowshed. Eve? The Lord alone knew where Eve was. 'She needs watching,' he said to the bells which were aiming in the general direction of heaven.

He fetched his knapsack from his room, helped himself to a piece of cheese to allay the pangs of hunger, and left 7/6d on the kitchen table to cover the cost of his weekend lodging.

It was a goodish walk to the bus-stop, along the cart-track to the lane, then a couple of miles of open tarmac, round the shoulder of Fossbury Beacon. It was hot, twenty yards ahead the surface of the road shifted like water.

Mel tipped his old boater over his eyes. He did not pause to look back for a last glimpse of the farm. He was envisaging the close of this chapter of his biography: 'The artist left Flinder's as he had arrived, without ceremony, and perhaps sooner than he intended. It was a compassionate decision: the impressionable young daughter of the house had fallen hopelessly in love with him. He, alas, had no such emotion to offer in return. He was wholly devoted to a lifelong mistress – his art. Rather than subject the girl to the pangs of unrequited love, he crept quietly away from the farm one afternoon in late summer, taking with him that inestimable body of work, the finest examples, it has been said, of his early pastoral phase . . .'

He rounded a bend in the lane and saw that someone was already at the stop. Someone looking his way, looking for the bus. Or for him.

Too late, he realised that the person was Eve. 'What the devil are you doing here?' He was asking himself, furiously, what lateness had to do with it.

'I came after you.'

He threw down his knapsack and stared at her. There was no call for dismay because there was no time between them – except past time.

'How did you manage to get here before me?'

'It's quicker along by the ditch.'

He saw where she had torn herself on brambles. The paper parcel she carried was torn, there were ball-burrs all over her coat.

'It's my best coat,' she said. 'You seen it now.'

'Where are you going?'

'I like your hat. My dad wore one the same when he got married.'

'Eve, you know you can't come with me.'

'Why can't I?'

'Get that idea right out of your head.' Little Sunday-go-to-meeting scarecrow in a maroon coat several sizes too big, bought, no doubt, for her to grow into. 'Where I'm going isn't suitable for children.'

'I'm not children. You wed me and I've got a ring.' She showed him. On the right finger of her left hand was a circle of plaited grass.

'You slay me,' said Mel. 'You don't believe that. Even you wouldn't believe that.' He could hear the bus approaching. It rounded the bend and he saw 'Salisbury' on the destination-board at the end of a list of intervening villages. 'Have you got any money?' Ten to one, no – twenty, no, he would bet a hundred to one, she had not. The bus drew alongside, a single-decker with wooden slat benches and a bicycle on the roof.

'Goodbye, Eve.' As he stooped and kissed her cheek she caught his arm. He shook her off. 'They'll put you in prison if you try to ride without paying.'

The driver sat at his wheel and took the fares as the passengers got on. Mel asked for a single to Salisbury.

He was stowing his knapsack away on the rack when he heard her say, 'My husband will pay. That's him in his wedding hat.'

THE TWICHILD

What stopped me in mid-flight was the fact that I didn't recognise him. He had been the love of my life twenty-five years ago, I haven't had another since and can't see myself doing so now at my age and with my current disposition. And I was in some sort of flight of fancies, dreams, and a fairly authentic and proportionate array of doctored memories at the prospect of seeing him again. 'Let's meet at the old place,' I said over the phone. 'The old place?' 'Deedie's, you remember Deedie's, or was it Dodie's?' He said no it wasn't Dodie's and yes, he remembered, but it wasn't like it used to be. He made a blowing noise down the wire, a sigh I supposed. 'It's become very rowdy.' So we arranged to meet in Marylebone High Street, a distinctly pricey area.

When I got to the restaurant, Scipio's or Scorpio's or whatever it was, someone was waiting outside. A bulky man in a melton topcoat and beaver hat. He had a stomach arc that belonged to the boardroom and I didn't give him a second glance, I marched into the restaurant looking for Hal.

A waiter came up and said yes, Mr Pritchard had reserved a table. 'Here he is now,' he said, and there was the beaver-hatted man right behind me.

That was the first rift in the lute. I might have guessed there'd be others, but I don't look for trouble, or for change. After twenty-five years I'm not looking for change. 'Hal!' I said, as if I'd only just seen him. I was staring at him with chronic disbelief. He had been a gaunt youth, raw-boned, with a tender skin and heavy eyelids, unfinished-looking, and said to be outgrowing his strength. He was fully finished now: if anything, he was overdone. Gone was the hungry look which I used to cherish because I was the only one, I thought I was, who could make it disappear. Gone was the mane of yellow hair which I used to comb with my fingers. He took off his hat and he had a few tabby strands disposed across his cranium. What I call stretch-covers. Harold Pritchard.

'Well,' he said, 'well.' It seemed to be all he could say and I did get a glimpse of the old way he used to open his eyes wide when he was moved.

I kissed him, not on his mouth, which had grown pursy, but on his cheek. Or rather his jowl. He had pale blue jowls. I was trying to believe that Hal Pritchard, my penurious love, was somewhere under the expense account charisma. I had to believe it if we were to have a meaningful encounter. Once there had been all the meaning in the world between us and I wasn't prepared to accept just a brush.

'Well,' he said again, 'you haven't changed much.'

I recommended he wait till he saw me in daylight. It's verifiably true that I have some down-lines and there are wrens' feet (not crows' as yet) under my eyes. I look shagged out on a bright British morning but fortunately there aren't many of those. The rest of me passes in not too refulgent lights. My skin and hair are OK and I work at my figure, and dentistry is an art in the States. I don't think I flatter myself if I say I'm still identifiable as the Kathy Waldeck who left these shores a quarter-century ago.

'Your usual table, Mr Pritchard,' said the waiter, divesting Hal of his coat. I could see Hal was a valued customer: a far cry from the days when we used to ask Deedie for outdated pies because they were cheap.

'It's been a long time.' Hal used not to make obvious remarks. Nor used he to have a wine list like a correspondence college diploma put into his hands. 'The usual for me, the Chevalier '53,' he said to the waiter. 'Madam will choose her wine later.'

'Madam will have the same as you,' I said. 'And a gin and ginger to start with. Is it sweet or sour, this Chevalier stuff?'

He used the wine list to waft the waiter away. 'It is a white burgundy, one of the best, and for me the most agreeable. Gastrically speaking.'

'Ulcers?' I said sympathetically.

'Not as yet.'

'In all other respects –' frankly, I didn't think he looked very fit – 'are you well?'

'Thank you, yes. And you?'

'Mercy's sakes –' my gin arrived on a salver – 'this is Kath, your old dolly-bird you're talking to, not the wife of the chairman. Or are *you* the chairman?'

'Not as yet,' he said again, with a quirk of the lips which I understood to mean that he was confidently expecting to top the board.

'I forget what you're into.'

'Into?'

'Your line of business.'

'We are ecclesiastical furnishers.'

'You mean church pews and things?'

'Everything from hassocks to altar cloths.'

'But it's not your scene, you were always heathen.'

'An agnostic. As I see it, my business is a logical extension of disbelief in the immaterial.' This time he did not quirk, he was solemn as a judge. 'Do you still like curry? They do an excellent chicken-liver pilau.'

'I'll have grapefruit, unsweetened, then a medium-rare steak, no vegetables, a side salad with a dressing of lemon juice and no onion.'

'Dieting?' said Hal.

'No. Just watching.'

'Let me see.' He frowned at the menu. 'Smoked salmon I think, then baked Suffolk ham with duchesse potatoes, brussels sprouts and string beans.'

It wasn't up to me to suggest that he should be watching too. I said, 'How's Jean?' because really it was Jean's fault. Had I married him I'd have kept tabs on his diet and he'd have been fifty pounds lighter.

'Fine.'

'Does she still do weaving?'

'No.'

That was a mercy. I remember her sitting, Penelope-like, at her loom. As soon as she got married she went into a homespun phase.

Literally. She made smocks and skirts and boleros of a sort of refined sacking, and wore them. She tried to get me to wear them. The colours were woad-blue or Lincoln-green, either way they looked terrible. I used to think she was trying to say something, like primitive is beautiful.

She'd had a funny upbringing in the non-comical sense. Her parents were so strait-laced that they didn't admit there was life below the navel. I wondered how they had ever got around to begetting Jean and when we were kids I decided she must be having a bad time because they saw her as their Sin that had to be expiated. And having married Hal who was brimming with Nature she might, I had decided, be trying to get herself right back to the source with her weaving.

'Dear old Jean,' I said, 'I'm dying to see her again.'

She had been my best friend. For the whole of the year of my affair with Hal she was away, working as a student teacher. She came home, saw Hal, Hal saw her and that was that. Love at first sight. She wasn't a raving beauty (nor was I), but she drove him wild with her segregated look, as if she'd been dusted off and put out of reach. I guess he thought she was in danger of being a saint. However, there was plenty of the old Eve in Jean.

'She never made enough of herself,' I said. 'Of her appearance, I mean. What does she wear now, now she's out of the merry peasant?'

He looked at me and I saw the fences going up. 'She wears clothes.'

'Ask a silly question.'

He turned away, snapped his fingers in the air. 'We're waiting for the Chevalier.'

What's this, I thought. We'd been lovers and I'd come home to look up old friends, of which he was the chiefest and oldest and suddenly I was being made to feel I had parity with the wine waiter who had forgotten the wine. 'I bet you don't even notice what she's got on,' I said. Next minute I wished I hadn't. He turned to me a face which showed that he was capable of making mincemeat of any bunch of hard-nosed businessmen and disgruntled shareholders.

I finished my gin and started on the grapefruit. Hal tasted the wine without making a ritual of it, for which I inwardly commended him.

'How are the children?'

'They're fine. Robin and David are at boarding-school and Beatrice is taking a commercial course.'

'Oh yes – Bea. How old is she now?'

'Sixteen.'

'Does she favour you or Jean?'

'Favour?'

'Take after. Look like.'

He sipped his wine and appeared to give the question thought. A change came over his face, it struck me that this was the first real expression I had seen on him this evening. 'She's not like either of us.'

'And the boys?'

'Are boys.'

'Well,' I said, more for something to be going on with and not taking special care, because I still thought that twenty-five years couldn't come between us, 'fathers usually prefer their daughters to their sons.'

'I love all my children,' he said, and the real live expression went out like a light switched off in his face. I felt put down and I said to myself I'd better mind my a's and b's, let alone my p's and q's.

But after that, the wine and food mellowed him and we talked about what I'd been doing, and America and England, and his parents who were still alive and kicking the Welfare State. I told him about my first husband, who had died, and the second one, who had ditched me.

'Ditched you?'

'He left me with no money and expensive tastes.'

'You should have married me.'

'I wanted to. You know that,' I said.

'Jean was pregnant.'

'You surprise me!' He did. I always thought she had played him with promises. But perhaps she saw that the bird in the hand would bring the one out of the bush. 'Oh well, that's the way the cookie's crumbled.'

And then he said, 'I didn't tell her I was coming to meet you.'

'Whyever not?'

'She'd have wanted to come.'

'Why shouldn't she come?' He shut his mouth, buttoned rather than pursed it, either way wasn't remotely characteristic of the Hal I had known. I said, 'I wanted her to come!' He inclined his head as if acknowledging a whim. 'Have you told her I'm here?'

'I shall tell her tonight.'

'What's she going to say when she knows we've met already?'

'Brandy is the logical conclusion to the meal, don't you think?' He snapped his fingers at the wine waiter.

'I've got to know what to say to Jean.'

'Brazilian or Turkish?'

'What?'

'Which coffee do you prefer?'

'I don't care if it's acorn.' I was angry. Jean was the friend of my youth and although we didn't correspond, we kept in touch – I thought we did – through Hal. Naturally I assumed he'd told her I was coming to England.

He ordered coffee and brandy and asked if I wanted to smoke. I put out my hand and as he lit our cigarettes he said, 'I wanted to see you alone.'

What was I to make of that? He wasn't giving me any sort of glad eye, he wasn't even looking at me. 'Any special reason?'

'I wanted to warn, or rather, to advise you.'

'She's not ill, is she?'

'No. But we don't go out together nowadays.'

'You mean you've split up?'

'Certainly not,' he said sharply and I thought he disapproves of divorce, he thinks marriage is till death us do part. I supposed it went with his job, I supposed there were some little hang-ups he had to accept even though he had suspended belief in things spiritual. 'But Jean has changed. You will see quite a difference.'

'I guess so. She'll see a difference in me.' And he, of all people, shouldn't think he'd got away with it. 'We all look twenty-five years older.'

'Jean doesn't.'

'That's great,' I said, 'that's terrific. If she's found a way to cheat Father Time I'll be delighted. Mind you, I'll want to know how she does it.' He looked at me as if I was still on the other side of the Atlantic. 'It doesn't explain why you're keeping her out of sight. Or is it *me* you're keeping out of sight?'

'You? I should have married you.'

'Maybe. But I'm longing to see Jean and the family. Can I come over on Sunday?'

'Come to lunch. The boys won't be home but Beatrice will.'

'Tell me, I'm so intrigued, how does Jean *look*?' I had a terrible, shattering thought and my stomach turned over. 'Hal, it's not – nothing bad's happened to her?'

'Bad?' he frowned. Somehow I was reassured by the way he put his chin on his hand and laid his finger across his lips. He seemed to be considering it for the first time, and if so, it couldn't be all that serious. 'I don't know what category of badness it would go into. Certainly not evil, or moral. And don't worry, it isn't horrific. I'm not even sure how wrong it is, relatively speaking. It is rather a matter of being not good. And then the question arises, not good for whom?'

'I don't understand.'

We looked at each other, he with a kind of disbelief which somehow included me. 'You must see for yourself.'

I couldn't rest between then and Sunday for wondering what I was going to find when I went to Mitcham, where they were living, on the edge of the Common. Suburban country, Hal called it. He offered to fetch me from Mitcham Station but I preferred to make my own way. I never know what time I'll retrieve consciousness in the mornings.

I was staying in West Central and by the time I'd breakfasted and got myself to Victoria and waited for a train and trundled through the hard crust of Wandsworth and Battersea to the terminus at Mitcham it was well past noon. I found a cab outside the station to take me the rest of the way. I like to walk if I know how far I've got to go and the weather's clement. But I didn't know and there was a leak in the air, between fog and rain, and with the penetrative power of both. The Common, as we drove across, looked just that, the bushes all public and the ground roughed up like a busted mattress. Where I live, if there's a bit of land idle it's because it's worth a billion dollars to someone to keep it so. Hal's and Jean's house – it was called 'Grassmead', a surprising bit of tautology – would probably be described by the realtor as 'enviably situated with privileged frontage and open view'. Frankly, I prefer bricks and mortar to grit walks and thorn bushes.

The first person I saw when I got out of the cab was one of the boys riding a bike round and round the apron-drive in front. He was sitting on the handlebars and pedalling backwards. That would be Robin, the youngest, I thought. How is it kids don't break their necks when they abuse the law of gravity?

I paid the cab and stood waiting for the child to come back on his circuit, which he did, and halted in front of me. By pedalling a half-turn forward and a half-turn back he managed to stay upright on the machine.

'Hi,' I said. 'You're Robin, aren't you?'

'Hallo, Kathy!' He stepped off with one easy movement, letting the bike fall to the ground and launched himself at me. Throwing his arms round my neck he cried, 'Oh it's so good to see you again!'

You know how it is when everything seems normal and if not actually predictable seems it can be predicated from the known facts and then all at once there are no facts, no normality, you realise you don't know the first thing and you get what amounts to a poke in the eye? If you've never had the experience you're either lucky or hardboiled.

'My God!' I was probably over-reacting and it certainly wasn't polite, but I couldn't stop myself. The bike-rider wasn't young Robin, it wasn't young, it wasn't a boy. It was Jean. My old, coming-up-to-fifty-year-old friend Jean. I remember her saying to me, and she couldn't have been more than eight years old at the time, 'You shouldn't be doing handstands at your age'. Stately, sober-sided – womanly. She was never a girl so much as a nun headed for the nunnery. She had the face for a wimple.

F5527

Now here she was, slender as a reed, half the size I remembered her, hair cropped and – yes, they were freckles, not gravespots, on her cheekbones, wearing a T-shirt, pre-shrunk jeans and dirty sandshoes.

She stood away from me, dashing the rain off her face, as excited – there was no other way to describe it – as a schoolkid. 'Kath, you haven't changed a bit!'

'You have,' I said, still not able to stop myself. She hugged me so hard that my handbag crushed my ribs.

Anyone as close to her as I was then would be in two minds about her age: mind number one aware of and marvelling at her aliveness and agility, mind number two noting the thickening of her skin, the lap of flesh under her throat and the flecks of grey in her hair.

'I've been waiting for you, I came out here so that I'd be the first to greet you.'

'I'm glad.' I was glad – of a chance to get a hold of myself. I needn't let them see I was in a state of shock, and worse, that I wasn't sure how shocked I ought to be. There was an element, if not of absurdity, of sheer incredulity about it. I saw it turning out to be some sort of practical joke, with the laugh on me and everyone crying 'We fooled you!' I thought, I mustn't show too much: obviously I've got to show something, but only enough to keep my dignity. No, I thought furiously, not my dignity, my self-respect. And then the next minute I wondered if Hal had sent her out in order to help me, or had she come herself, knowing – she must know – what a shock it would be? I was in considerable confusion all round, and when she said, 'Come on indoors,' I again couldn't stop myself and I said, 'Aren't you going to pick up your bike?'

As soon as we went in I knew there was something wrong, or rather, I knew that what was wrong had got into the house, right down into the carpets. Everyone knows how a house looks when it's not being cared about. This one showed signs of having been pretty exhaustively cared about in the past: there were Afghan slip-rugs, copper troughs of grape-ivy, feather-fern and crotons, Dutch tiles and horse-brasses over the chimney-breast, finger plates on the doors, tapestries – done by Jean probably – on the walls. It was what I would have expected of Jean.

But there was something resigned and ignored about it all. The plants were dusty and unkempt, the brasses tarnished, the slip-rugs had slipped out of their functional places. The furniture stood around being furniture, not required and not looking prepared to serve any purpose. Someone, a daily probably, hoovered in an unvarying circle round the floor and dabbed the dust off the living-surfaces, but I could see saucers of fluff round the feet of immovables like the sideboard and the breakfront bookcase.

I'm not houseproud, my place gets in a mess and stays that way until I find the urge to clean up. If Jean had been even remotely like her old self I would have blinked an eye. Everyone's entitled to an off-day and I wouldn't expect her to polish the stair-rods because I was coming.

Then when I saw Hal's face I thought if he sent her out he did it for himself, not for me. Hal was going to bluff it through. He had his company director's face on, it was not just smooth, it was impermeable.

'Kathy.' He reached for my hand and kissed it.

That was another shock, in reverse, because he always used to kiss my hand when we met. Just as I had decided that I wasn't going to get a glimpse of the old Hal today, he had to go and do something which had been outwardly playful yet essentially private and meaningful to ourselves.

'I thought we were never going to see you again,' said Jean. 'I didn't think you'd want to come back.'

'My roots are here.' It wasn't true, I don't have roots, it was just something I'd heard people say and it could be what I was supposed to say now. Supposition was all I had to go on.

'You never even came for a visit.'

'I wanted to, but you know how it is.'

'No, how is it?'

'Things pile up, and people. This is the first chance I've had to get away. It's no good coming for a weekend, is it?'

'People?' she said. '*People* pile up?'

[23]

'We mustn't question Kathy's motives,' said Hal.

A young girl came in, Hal's daughter, the first of his children I had actually seen, and she at least was what I would have expected before I discovered how random expectation can be. She was a typical school-girl, with very long, very fine brown hair the way they all wear it, straight as a yard of pump-water as my mother used to say, a skin like buttermilk and a figure at the uncoordinated stage. There wasn't a lot she could have done with herself but I've seen what kids have done when they've tried and I was glad she hadn't.

'Why, Bea,' I said. 'It *is* Bea, isn't it?' She held out her hand, shyly, and I took her by the shoulders and kissed her. 'I'm happy to know you.'

'Would you like to come upstairs? You must be tired after your journey.'

I was grateful, no one else had suggested I even take my coat off. She took me into one of the front bedrooms. There were two single beds but only one set of brushes on the dressing-table, and a flask of aftershave with Christmas tinsel still round the neck.

Bea watched me while I fixed my hair. 'I expect you're used to travelling.'

'Not by British Rail.'

'If you want to wash –' whether she intended it or not, it sounded like a sequitur – 'the bathroom is across the passage.'

'Is this your parents' room, Bea?'

'My name's Beatrice.' She smiled. 'Shall I call you Aunt?'

'As you like.'

'Aunt Kate.'

'Why not Kathy?'

'Kathy doesn't suit you.'

So how did I like that, after forty-odd years? I didn't. I stopped in the act of giving myself a new mouth and looked at her in the mirror. 'Beatrice suits *you*.'

'I like it,' she said calmly. 'Do you want to see the house?'

'I guess your mother will show me round.'

'I didn't answer your question.'

'What question was that?'

'This is Daddy's room and this –' she opened a communicating door – 'is hers.'

I went and looked in. I saw all I needed and a whole lot more than I wanted in about one minute. I don't usually blaspheme, and not in front of children, but I couldn't stop myself. Blasphemy seemed like the only rational reaction.

'I'm sorry,' I said, 'I don't understand what's going on.'

'I expect you could do with a cup of tea.'

'I could do with something stronger.'

We went downstairs and the first thing she said was, 'Aunt Kate would like a gin and ginger, Daddy.'

'How did you know?' I said.

'A hostess makes it her business to know that sort of thing.'

After that I knew I didn't wholly like this Beatrice.

Hal was standing in the same place, the same attitude, as when we left him to go upstairs. I don't think he had moved a muscle. Jean was sitting on the edge of the table, swinging her legs. She jumped down and ran at me, seizing my waist and whirling me round and round. 'I'm so glad you're here!'

At that moment I was anything but glad to be there. I'd like to have been some place quiet by myself, to figure out what was happening. With Jean spinning me round and laughing and me trying to keep my feet I was completely hazed. Also I was dizzy and I know I looked like some sort of big bobbin. Jean was crazy with excitement and – even at that moment I knew it – sheer joy at seeing me. Then I lost my footing and was about to go down on my butt. I clutched her as I went and we both fell into a chair. There we were, Jean over my knees as if I was about to give her a spanking.

Hal watched us from behind his business face. Beatrice had a small withdrawn smile somewhere, so withdrawn I couldn't actually see it, but I knew it was directed at me. Her I *could* have spanked.

Jean got out of my lap and sat cross-legged on the floor beside me.

'Dear Kath, you're the one who went away and you're the one who hasn't changed.'

I got the message; I saw that she believed, she needed to believe, that some things don't change, that there was a norm – *I* needed to believe that – which she could get back to. I was remembering that room of hers.

Hal brought my drink, silently handed it to me. Beatrice said, 'Do make yourself comfortable, Aunt Kate,' which I took – perhaps I was being unduly sensitive – as a reference to the inelegant way I had collapsed into the chair. 'I have things to do in the kitchen. Lunch won't be long.'

Hal poured himself a large whisky. We were all in need of something. 'Is Bea doing the cooking?'

He nodded. 'She's good at it.'

'I'll have a coke,' said Jean.

'Are you on the wagon?' I said to her.

'I don't like the stuff you're drinking, it gives me a headache.'

'Are you OK, honey? Not sick or anything? You've lost weight.'

'I never felt better. I'm fit as a flea and I eat like a horse. You'll see.'

I did. Sunday lunch was on the table prompt at one: roast sirloin, baked and boiled potatoes, cauliflower and individual Yorkshire puddings. The meat was a fine shade of russet with pinky depths, the cauliflower white and tender, the potatoes crisp, the puddings brown puffballs cleft to show their golden hearts. It was served in nice old Worcester dishes that would have fetched a small fortune in New York.

'I must congratulate you, Bea,' I said.

'Must you?' Definitely I wasn't being hypersensible, but she made it sound as if I grudged her the praise. 'I thought you'd like a traditional English meal.'

Hal carved, Bea was opposite him at the other end of the table. Jean and I faced each other across it and I had ample opportunity to notice how good her appetite was. She was a simple assembly and disposal unit, she mashed everything up together and ate through. She looked up at me from chasing the gravy over the Worcester birds with the end of her knife, 'Did you come on Concorde?'

'No.'

'A DC-10?'

'I wouldn't know. It was something with wings.'

'Sometimes I go to Heathrow and stay all day.'

'Whatever for?'

'To watch the planes.'

Hal filled my glass. His hand was steady. 'Beaujolais nouveau. I thought it would go with the beef.'

'Do you like living in America, Aunt Kate?' said Beatrice. I nodded. 'Why?'

I could have told her, there were reasons, and I could have been specific. But it was personal to me, and I didn't fancy explaining myself to young Beatrice. 'I like living.'

'I don't think I'd fit in. Do you, Daddy?'

'It's a big country,' I said. 'You'd find a corner.'

She looked at Hal and smiled like one of those young matrons in old Dutch paintings and he looked at her and suddenly I not only wanted to knock their heads together, I knew I ought to.

'I'm going to America,' said Jean.

'You are?' I was surprised and delighted. 'That's great! Hal didn't tell me.' He was addressing himself – that was the only word for it – to his plate. 'You must come and stay with me.' Yes, that was the answer, I'd get her over this phase, whatever it was. 'I'll show you New York. Manhattan, Fifth Avenue, Broadway – we'll have a wonderful time.'

'I'd like to see the Boston Sabres.'

'The what?'

Jean's eyes shone. 'The best ice-hockey team ever!'

Then a sickening thing happened. Beatrice said, and it was the first time I'd heard her speak directly to her mother, 'Did you wash your hands before coming to the table?' Jean promptly hid her hands below the tablecloth. 'Let me see,' said Beatrice. Jean glowered. 'Then go and do it now. At once.' There was a long pause. I was begging Jean, silently, to tell Beatrice to go to hell. But she stood up and went like a graceless child.

I couldn't eat after that. Beatrice raised her eyebrows when I refused the sweet. Hal said, 'It's gooseberry tart, Beatrice has a good hand with pastry.'

'Perhaps Aunt Kate has to be careful what she eats.'

'I guess something upset me,' I said.

Beatrice served coffee in what she was pleased to call the 'lounge', speaking the word roundly and innocently. I would have been amused if I hadn't disliked her so much. It was absurd, of course, to take against a child, because that was all she was, but there was the other child, there was Jean, who had been sent to the bathroom.

'Isn't she coming back?' I said.

Beatrice shrugged. Hal started to his feet. 'I'll fetch her.'

'No,' I said quickly, 'I'll go.'

She was in her room, the room that had so shocked me. I can still see it, I'll never forget it, it still makes me want to cry.

'Jean, can we talk?'

She was lying on the bed, a narrow bunk-bed with a bright Indian blanket, her hands clasped under her neck. I don't think she'd washed, there were grease marks on her elbows.

The walls of the room were smothered with pictures of pop stars: I had to believe that's what they were, all those freaked-out creatures with contorted faces and hair like the staple diet of horses. Over the bed was a Dracula mask, on the chest of drawers a collection of model cars.

I made myself look at everything, I kept hoping I'd find a clue among the cricket stumps, the footballs, skateboard, boxing-gloves and spotters' charts. I picked up the gloves, they were well used. 'You don't –?'

'They're David's.'

I was so thankful, thinking I could see daylight and maybe beyond that, reason. 'So this is David's room?'

'It's my room. Do you like it?' She knew I didn't and she didn't wait for an answer. 'I'd love to learn to box but no one will teach me. David flatly refused. But I'm learning judo and skin-diving and I practice dribbling on my own.'

'*Dribbling?*'

'For a pass. Like this.' She rolled off the bed and danced about, chasing an imaginary ball.

I caught her arm and held her. 'What's this all about?'

'About?'

'It's because of the boys, isn't it? Because they're away at school and you're missing them.'

'Yes and no I miss them,' she said calmly. 'There's more going on when they're here. But nothing's because of them. Nothing's because of anything.' That seemed, even to her, to need clarification. 'At least, not anything you'd know about.'

'Try me.'

I think she wanted to. But she couldn't, she never could have told me in words how it had started and gone on, building up inside her all her life, a life she'd been just waiting through. I did have some sort of inkling, picked up here and there from the past and ratified, you might say, by the present.

Not that it made me sympathetic, it made me mad. 'Think about the boys! Don't you ever wonder what they make of it?'

'I more or less know. David doesn't approve of me playing football. Robin doesn't mind, he's teaching me rugby tackles.' I shuddered. 'And I'm going caving.'

'Jean, what are you playing at?'

'It isn't a game, it's serious.' So was she, and reproachful. 'Spelae-ology is the scientific exploration of caves. You have to be trained and you wear a helmet and mask underground. I've always wanted to do it.'

'And this – this boy's stuff,' I gestured round the room, 'have you always wanted this?'

'I want to live my life.'

I could have thrown my head back and howled. I said, 'You and I were at school together and I'm forty-nine if I'm a day. We're pushing fifty, honey, we've darned near pushed it. Given a 75-year maximum term we've had the best part of our lives.'

'The best part?'

'Quantitatively speaking, we've had the big end.'

'I haven't.'

'You've had – you have – a husband and three kids.'

'Where does that leave me? It's not me, none of them is me!' She flung away into a corner of the room.

'If it's not you, if those kids aren't you, you and Hal, then what is, for heaven's sakes?'

'I've done nothing. Nothing of my *own*.' She swung round. 'It's all to do!' and she wasn't joyful or hopeful, she was in a crying rage. What could I say? That it was a nice idea, but she was short of time? Should I ask what she had in mind to do? Make a career? As the only menopausal lady footballer in the World Cup team? Climb Everest? Go to the moon? 'I'm going to show you, I'll show you all!'

Her face had that dangerous glitter before the floodgates open. But when she ran out of the room I was the one who shed tears. I heard the front door slam and the next thing was the sound of that damned bicycle being ridden round and round on the gravel.

I repaired my face and went downstairs. Hal was alone, so I came right out with it: 'How long has she been like this?' If he had said, 'Like what?' I'd have walked out of the house without another word. It would have been a whole lot better for me if he had, and I had.

'Over a year. Ever since the boys went away.'

'Do you think she's trying to compensate in some way?'

'I think she wants to have her life over again.'

'Hal, what she wants is someone else's life. If she was trying to have her own it would be as a girl, not a boy.' He sat pressing the tips of his fingers together and not quite smiling. 'Either way,' I said wretchedly, 'she's out of her cotton-picking mind.'

'It may seem to her that boys have the better time. Beatrice is of a different disposition. She and Jean were never very close.' I understood *that*. 'I have wondered,' he did not hide his distaste, 'if it's due to her time of life.'

'Has she seen a doctor?'

'She isn't physically ill. I went myself to discuss it with a psychiatrist, but of course he could do nothing without her co-operation.'

[30]

'And she won't co-operate?'

'She no longer talks, or acts, like a woman.' He looked at me, then his eyes slid away, and uneasily to and fro. 'Or a wife.'

'Hal.' I took his hand, sorry for him; his fingers, I was thinking, were pressed together in desperation.

He sighed. 'It has been a problem business-wise.'

'Business-wise?'

'There are social commitments attaching to my job, to the position I hold in the firm. Ours is a very sensitive business. One must be seen to be a celibate bachelor or irreproachably married. Reproach, however incurred, is bad for our image.' He was now quite smiling, in a thin, draw-string way. 'I am expected to preside with my wife, or to have her beside me. I am obliged to excuse Jean, of course.' Of course. Dinner at Lambeth Palace, lunch with the Archdeacon, all very Barchester Towers, and Jean in her jeans. I saw his difficulty. 'Sometimes I take Beatrice. Beatrice —' I thought he dwelled on the name – 'can be relied upon.'

That too I could see: Beatrice sitting on her hair among the bishops.

'It's just a phase, Jean's always had phases.' I noticed how crisp I sounded, taking confidence from my own confidence, a sort of cannibalism that seemed the only help. 'I guess you're right about her time of life. It happens and one never knows what form the symptoms will take, or for how long. But it will pass and everything will be the same again.'

'The same as what?'

Beatrice stood in the doorway. She had on a pinafore with a stand-up frill which went over her shoulders and under her bosom. Hers was a bold, not to say presumptive, young bosom and the effect of the frill was at once daring and demure. She was smiling, she knew fine what I meant.

I said, 'Can I help with the dishes?'

'We have a washing-up machine, Aunt Kate. Me.'

'I feel bad about leaving it all.'

'I'm used to it. Aren't I, Daddy?' She perched on the arm of his chair, looking down at the top of his head and disposing a strand of his hair that had become undisposed. 'I've got used to a lot of things.'

There they sat, Hal and his daughter, and as he gazed up at her, widening his eyes as he always had when he was moved, I saw, through the extra flesh he had put on over the years, the raw bones of the Hal I had known. And I saw something else I had known – his hungry look.

AN EXCELLENT THING IN A WOMAN

He had never before witnessed such an exhibition – if he could call such an essentially private in-fight that – and was sufficiently distracted by it to neglect to change down in time for a corner. Having to do so in the act of bringing the car off the straight was a piece of bad driving which crystallised his displeasure.

Kathy was saying, 'If I don't think about you you cease to exist.'

'What you mean is, you're always occupied with trivia.'

'Hours of annihilation, weeks of non-being. Your life could be written on a postage stamp!'

'Try to think a little each day, just for my sake.'

'I may as well tell you I can't think of you as a graduate. What will you do, my poor love, without a degree?'

'Learn hypnotherapy from Aunt Rosie and elope with the richest of her bandaged bitches.'

They laughed and Dennis said he thought they were fussing Hugh.

'I never do that.' Kathy leaned against Hugh, her breast touching his hand on the wheel.

'Obviously you do more,' Dennis smiled confederately into the driving-mirror, 'or he wouldn't have to marry you.'

Hugh ignored the smile. 'We'll go via Witney, it's rather pleasant.'

'Will there be a chance to look at the Blanket Hall?'

'Oh,' cried Kathy, 'he's trying to be amusing and he's no good at it. We laugh at his jokes so that he won't feel deprived.'

'I feel deprived on other counts.' Dennis leaned over from the back seat and put his arms round her throat. 'You don't entirely compensate me, sister mine.'

'How can I when you have so many natural disadvantages?'

'I once took a rubbing of a brass in the church of St Mary the Virgin.

It was 14th century, rather beautiful, and I meant to have it on my Christmas cards, but the block came out subtly different and really rather sinister. Do you know –' Dennis was looking into the driving-mirror, talking to Hugh – 'it was like an impermeable cobweb.'

'I'm not surprised,' said Kathy. 'You don't believe in God.'

Hugh eased his foot steadily down on the accelerator. 'We can't linger in Witney, lunch will be waiting for us.'

Turning in her seat, Kathy saw the road and the wide-awake spires being paid out behind them and cried to Dennis, 'I wish you were coming!'

She was in one of her abysses which it was Hugh's pleasure and privilege to pluck her out of. No one was ever so swiftly dismayed as Kathy nor so deliciously reassured.

'They'd see through us,' Dennis said. 'My disadvantages would not detract from yours.'

Hugh gripped the wheel. His hands were tied, his perception, though not blunted, was unemployable. 'We're going for the weekend, not a character assessment.'

'At least they would see there are two of us,' Kathy said sorrowfully.

Hugh had actually been relieved at Dennis's appearance. Having prepared himself for some androgynous figure in flowered trousers, he found the boy's pink shirt and outsize tie and tendrils of curling hair not personally offensive. Dennis would pass unexcepted in a crowd.

'Why won't you come?' wailed Kathy.

'I haven't been asked.'

Hugh somehow had the impression that their faces were complementary – required of each other for the full statement of their personalities. It was absurd, of course. A fine prospect if it were not! If it were not, he would himself be similarly incomplete without his sister. Rather the reverse was true, he sometimes felt that Cecile would overdo anything that he did.

'Perhaps you'd like to come to lunch on Sunday?' Trying not to sound driven to ask, he threw the invitation over his shoulder and out of the window.

[34]

'Sunday wil

'What?'

'I shall be

'Sunday

and walk

imagine h

'Wha

agreed

He br

al mi

Den

c

black girl ra

would look at them an

Displeased, Hugh stared anu

ing tar, and decided to return via Woodsto

'But Hugh would always look at me.' She pusheu

thigh and for the second time he forbore to remonstrate witn

hampering his gear movements.

Sam told him that he was lucky. 'By God you are! With that figure –
what a vessel!' Sam was like a dodgem-car, rushing and ramming.
'Those legs and bosom – luscious I call her, and that buttoned-up
mouth, she's a natural tease and – I'm right, aren't I – a quick starter?'

'She's not a horse.' Hugh met and held Sam's stare. 'Please spare us
any obvious analogies.'

'Has she anything coming to her besides . . .' Sam grinned. 'Besides?'

'I don't know.'

'Oh yes you do. You've got a damn
Spenlow if you hadn't. I married one,
Hugh frowned. Cecile's choice of
standably, to an out-going nat
containment. He himself was d
But in choosing Sam Purdi
should be a balanced rela
time.
'Kathy has a broth
could add, 'I've ask
Weston Priory.'
'You'll make
the best of th
time I shor
Sam
drinki
San
as

good idea, you wouldn't be a
emember.'
a life partner had turned, under-
ure in contrast to her own self-
rawn to Kathy on the same principle.
e, Cecile had overcompensated. What
tionship had become the battle of a life-

r.' Why did he say that? Presumably so that he
ed him over to lunch tomorrow. He's staying at

out better than I did, you're bound to. Mind you, I got
e bargain when your sister married me – it was the one
t-changed the Spenlows.'
usted out something stronger than the light sherry they were
g and Hugh lifted his nose out of range. He felt a little sorry for
because Cecile had chosen him for his extroversion and that was
near as she could get to love.

She came in, tall and sandy, wearing a brilliant magenta dress that showed her knees. Hugh knew those knees, he had them himself. While he was still in short trousers those same patellas had earned him the nickname of 'Fruitlegs'.

Cecile, in short skirts, did not inspire a nickname. She looked fantastic in a ceremonial way, contriving to be at once in the fashion and outside the comedy.

'When Kathy comes down we'll have lunch.' She smiled. 'Well, Hugh?'

'Well?' He said eagerly, 'Do you like her?'

'We've only just met.'

'What are your first impressions? You always say they're the most important.'

'She seems a nice child.'

'Child? She's twenty-two.'

'A perfect age.'

[36]

'What don't you like about her?'

'My dear, have I said I don't?'

Sam winked. 'Committee's still in session.'

'Silly lad.' Cecile touched Hugh's cheek with a gesture she had not been able to use for years.

At lunch Kathy made the mistake of encouraging Sam. She let herself be swept along – with encouragement Sam was a world-sweeper. His partisanship was a liability but Kathy couldn't seem to see where the balance of power was and that her tender best interests were being disserved. As Hugh watched her foundering he could have appreciated Cecile's usage of Sam, marvelled at her cleverness in marrying him. She must have foreseen his potentialities, what a tool to her hand he would be, what an agent, what a weapon. But he was too involved in what was being done to admire how it was done.

Kathy was enjoying herself. She swallowed Sam's jokes whole, and neglected, for laughter, the excellent cold soufflé Cecile had prepared. She shared Sam's digs and innuendoes, even those aimed at Cecile. Didn't she know that that was unforgiveable and always would be, however long she was married into the family?

'Is this the first time you've been vetted? You're taking it well,' said Sam.

'I've been engaged before, but privately.'

'Privately?'

'We didn't tell anyone. There wasn't time, we broke it off the next day.'

Cecile raised her brows. 'I see.'

'Oh no you couldn't,' Kathy said seriously. 'We were madly un-suited.'

'Ah well, it's a gamble,' said Sam. 'You marry for love and find you've got a life contract for mowing the lawn.'

'How did you know you were unsuited?' Cecile helped Sam to more soufflé. She looked serenely domestic but Hugh divined her purpose and her intimation before she made it. He wanted to tell Kathy to choose a safe answer. But what was safe?

[37]

NO WORD OF LOVE

'I had a revelation,' said Kathy, 'and so did he. We discovered afterwards that it came to us both at exactly the same moment. Like being struck by lightning.'

'How satisfactory.' Cecile smiled. 'So it wasn't a reasoned decision? You didn't give it thought?'

She hadn't bothered to conceal the trap. Why should she? Kathy wasn't expecting a trap, she wouldn't even know when she fell into it and only Hugh and Cecile would hear it sprung.

'I did put it to a scientific test and the answer was negative. You see, I couldn't use his toothbrush.'

'What?'

'It's infallible.' Kathy looked from Cecile to Sam. 'Just ask yourselves, could you use one another's toothbrushes?' She said warmly, 'I'm sure you could. It's absolutely fundamental. Much more so than sharing beds or bodies. I mean, what secrets could you have or want to have from someone as close to you as that?'

Sam slapped his knee. 'Coupled in a denture bath! That's way-out sex for you!'

Cecile asked, 'Could you use Hugh's?'

'Yes, I could.'

'And he's so finicky that if he could use yours it would certainly prove something –' Cecile laughed – 'though I'm not sure what.'

Hugh threw down his table-napkin. 'For heaven's sake, let's have no more of this nonsense.'

'What an advertising gimmick! The toothbrush as sex symbol.' Sam looked solemn. 'But is there too much permissiveness? Too much sharing would mean a drop in sales.'

'I said that's enough!'

'Can't you take a joke, dear?' Sandily smiling, Cecile had always been able to undermine Hugh; at an early age he had learned not to build on sand.

'We aren't all joking.'

By tea time Kathy was despondent. 'She doesn't like me.'

'Of course she does.'

'You can't see it but I can. Women know these things by instinct.'

They were walking in the garden and she bowed herself under the Japanese quince. 'You don't like me either!'

'All right, I don't. But I love you and you'll have to be content with that.'

'What can I do to make her like me?'

'It's not important whether she does or not.'

'It is to you. Oh can't we go? Can't we go away from here now?'

'Don't be ridiculous, of course we can't.' Exasperated, he watched her wilt, she wilted like the fleshiest flower deprived of water. 'There's one thing you can try not doing. Don't laugh at Sam's jokes.' He said, disgusted at the thinness of the lie: 'She may be a little jealous that you seem to like him best.'

'Well I do.' Kathy dragged off the head of a snapdragon. 'At least he's honest.'

After dinner they played bridge. They invariably did when Hugh stayed the weekend. Sam brought out the cards as soon as the dishes were cleared.

'You know this game, girlie?'

Kathy shook her head.

'That's a shame. I thought we'd have a fourth for once.'

Cecile, to do her justice, offered them the chance of doing something else.

'Why don't you two go for a walk? Hugh, show Kathy our river, or stroll along to the Ring of Bells.'

He thought she would be glad to get away, but she said firmly, 'I'd rather stay here.'

She had made up her mind to something. To what? To keep to the letter of the law – his law as she now chose to regard it – in the hope that the spirit might be induced to turn up later. My little amorist, he thought, it won't work, not with you, not with Cecile.

'Of course she'd rather!' boomed Sam. 'Why would she want to go out in the dark with Hugh? Don't tell me, don't anyone tell me. Let me keep some illusions.'

'As you wish,' Cecile said to Kathy, 'Do you want to look at television?'

'I haven't brought my glasses. I do have them, one eye's long-sighted and the other's short-sighted and it's such a fight to adjust to television that I get a headache.'

'We'll play three-handed as usual.' Sam was shuffling the cards.

'Perhaps Kathy wants to talk.'

'Oh no!' Alarmed, she obviously took it for an injunction. 'I've nothing to talk about, I mean there's nothing I want to.'

Usually Hugh enjoyed bridge with Cecile and Sam. They were good players and took the game seriously. Tonight he couldn't concentrate, he couldn't even take it as a game. As he picked up his hand he realised that he had been improvident. The disposition — three of them occupied and isolated, Kathy adrift and over-anxious — was not favourable. He should have foreseen how it could turn out: Cecile would not need to lift a finger.

Kathy walked about the room carrying her glass. She leaned on his shoulder to look at his cards.

'Is that good? Is it a Grand Slam?'

'If you're marrying into the family you'd better learn to play,' said Sam. 'Come here and I'll show you the rudiments.'

Hugh said, 'Kathy, wouldn't you rather go out?'

'I wouldn't and it's rude of you to suggest it.'

She was looking at him with fierce dispassion over the rim of her glass. He wondered how much she would drink to help achieve whatever she thought she could achieve.

'Hugh, Kathy's glass is empty,' Cecile said. 'At least see that she has a drink.'

He appreciated the 'at least'. My sister, you bitch, he thought and poured Kathy a very little gin.

'I'm glad Dennis can come to lunch,' she was saying. 'It was nice of you to invite him.'

'Hugh did that.' Cecile smiled. 'Of course we want to meet your brother.'

Kathy giggled. 'Hugh was conned into it, Dennis can always get what he wants.'

'And you?' Cecile said gaily, 'Cannot you always get what you want?'

'No.'

Kathy's stare went through them to the world beyond. What disenchantments was she reviewing? Had she been disabused at the beginning, born with the after-taste of honey in her mouth? Hugh ached for her, knowing how little she actually wanted for herself and that her modest hopes were what most people took as their right.

Sam nudged him. 'Are you playing or dreaming?'

He hadn't looked at his hand and when he did he felt like throwing the cards on the table.

'No bid.'

'Three no trumps,' said Sam. 'There'll be a damn good dummy.'

Kathy spoke over their heads to Cecile. 'Dennis isn't like me, he's clever. Sometimes I have to forget him entirely, I make myself put him right out of my mind, it's as if he's never lived.'

'Why?'

'Oh not for bad reasons – for the best. You'll like him.'

If she could think that, what hope was there? Whom did she trust? Dennis? Cecile?

'I do want to talk, don't I?' She herself refilled her glass to the rim. 'About Dennis. You see – you will see – he's completely sufficient. It wouldn't matter what came up –' she drank and rushed on, gesturing with the half-empty glass – 'I've seen him go into rooms full of people, total strangers, and twist them round his little finger. It's a wonderful accomplishment.'

'Twisting is?' Cecile smiled.

'They don't know they're even bending, they think the world is going round *them*, they like it.' She said to herself with her sudden and absolute dismay, 'Oh God.'

'Isn't it odd to want to forget your brother?'

'My brother – that's the point.'

Sam grunted and stared at his cards. He didn't see the point. Did Cecile?

Cecile said softly, 'I never want to forget Hugh.'

'Nor do I. And if I were you I shouldn't need to.'

Hugh went to her and took the glass out of her hand. 'I think you had better go to bed.'

'I must tell them about Dennis!'

'You've told them. And tomorrow they'll see for themselves.'

'What will they see?' He pulled her to her feet and she clung to him gladly, even at that moment he could feel the unquenchable, separate gladness her body had in his. 'I've got to explain about Dennis and me –'

'They'll see that you have no faith in us.'

'Us?'

'I'm marrying you.'

If that was something she still wondered at she was currently overtaken by other wonders and so had been relieved of it for the time being. 'Well, you can't marry Dennis,' she said, and smiled groggily at Cecile from under his ear. He got her upstairs. She protested, she was thinking, with the gin to help her, that there were good words she could put in for herself. He made her lie on the bed. She clasped her hands round his neck and held him.

'Stay with me!'

'I can't. Close your eyes.' He gently pressed down her lids, not liking her blurred and desperate stare. 'Try to sleep a little.'

'You'll come back? Tonight?'

'Good heavens, no, not here. It's out of the question.'

'But I need you!'

'I need you, but this is my sister's house.'

Kathy's eyes flicked wide open as soon as he removed his fingers. 'Doesn't she ever need anyone?'

'She wouldn't admit it.'

When he reappeared downstairs, Sam said, 'What about this game?'

'I'm going to marry her!'

Cecile smiled. 'So we understand.'

[42]

'Why don't you like her?'

'My dear, what is there to dislike?'

'I want a fair answer.'

'Then you should ask a fair question. I do like her and I'm asking you why shouldn't I?'

'She's a nice kid,' said Sam. 'A bit silly.'

Cecile took her place at the card-table and picked up the hand Sam dealt her. 'She's immature. Time will remedy that.'

'But you doubt it,' said Hugh. 'You very much doubt it. Some people never mature, they never make good wives and mothers, they never make women. To the end of their days you have to tremble for them at parties, cover up for them, opt out for them, get your family to shrug –'

'I never shrug, neither does Sam.'

'Stuffy of me,' Hugh said bitterly, 'but I don't find it amusing.'

Cecile threw down her cards. 'Very well, since you ask me I'll tell you. I think you're the one with doubts and I think that poor child knows it.'

Kathy, who had followed him downstairs and was standing in the doorway asked, 'Please can I have a drink of water?'

She had a headache next morning but was blindingly cheerful. They all found it a strain, like being obliged to follow the bobbing of a ping-pong ball on a jet of water. She was remotest and brightest with Hugh so that he began to feel he ought to semaphore to her. It was patently absurd and he was torn between rage and pity. Cecile maintained a bogus gravity towards them both. Sam winked.

There was nothing he could do. Talking had never been a satisfactory method of communication between them. And he could not speak to her or comfort her in the way they understood, not here in his sister's house. It was not a matter of principle, it was a matter of fact.

He had to watch the skin paper-thin with pain across her forehead, and listen to her knocking tack after tack into her coffin. When she thought he wasn't looking she gazed up at him from the depths of her abyss. He made no mistake, he it was who had consigned her there.

After breakfast he suggested she sit in the garden. He thought that there would only be Sam blundering about with a pair of shears and she could then stop destroying herself for appearance's sake. Or would she sit smiling at the crack of a twig and the rustle of an insect?

Relief was not something he felt in connection with Dennis, he was simply thankful to get away for a while and he drove to Weston Priory with the intention of stopping for a quiet drink before he fetched the boy. He had forgotten that Dennis was walking to meet him.

When he drew up before the inn which was less than half way to Weston, there was Dennis sitting on the bench outside. Hugh was wretchedly angry, with Dennis for being there and with himself for being so irrational as to find it the last straw. When Dennis greeted him he could only manage to nod in reply.

'I thought I'd flag you as you passed. Isn't it a marvellous morning?' Dennis said happily, 'I've been here an hour with my one half pint.'

'You'll have another?'

'I have to warn you I'm skint, I shan't be able to stand you one.'

Hugh walked away and Dennis ran after him shaking a wasp out of his empty tankard.

'What must it be like to be an insect and stoned? All those legs and proboscis to cope with, to say nothing of wings. Don't drink and fly. And if you settle to sleep it off you get swatted. I'm glad I'm human, aren't you?'

Hugh remembered Kathy saying how sufficient Dennis was. This morning her absurdity was terminal. He cursed softly.

'Is anything wrong?'

'Should there be?'

'No. I suppose,' said Dennis, watching him push his empty glass back across the bar, 'you always drink double whiskies.'

'Have you any objection?'

'No, I think it's rather gorgeous.'

Hugh looked at him sharply. He was perched on a stool, chin in hand, a half pint of bitter at his elbow. He seemed serious, he also seemed not to think he had said anything exceptionable. Hugh, who wished to take exception, found that he could not.

'What's gorgeous about it?'

'Why, being able to afford it!'

Hugh pointed to Dennis's tankard. 'Are you going to drink that?'

'Oh, I've learned to like beer.' He sipped it cheerfully. 'How's Kathy?'

'She has a headache.'

Dennis nodded. He had either anticipated it or hadn't been listening.

'I'm terribly glad you asked me over. You've saved me from a gruesome afternoon. They eat stupefying Sunday roasts at the Priory and lie down to sleep it off until tea time. Then they get up and live a little – watching television.'

'You won't find us such swinging company either.'

'You *are* bushed. It must be Kathy.'

'Why the devil should it be Kathy?' Hugh's anger exploded. Surely here was the right target, here was Kathy's own substance, her same genetic mixture. 'I'll tell you what it is – you're all against her, even you. That's how it started, her own family started it. She was brought up to mistrust herself. The only peace she gets is what I give her.' He said furiously, not caring if Dennis divined how that peace was besᵻ ved, 'She does know then that she's doing the right thing!'

'You're wrong – about the family, I mean.' Dennis's gaze was substantially the same as Kathy's but it developed differently – or should one merely say it developed? 'We work like mad to convince her she's as good as we are. And you know what I think? The conclusion I've come to is that she really thinks she's a whole lot better.'

'She probably is.' Hugh marched to the door.

Dennis picked up his tankard. 'Can we sit in the garden while I drink this? It's awfully hot in here.'

Hugh would rather have not. He had no wish to prolong the tête-à-tête, it was not serving any useful purpose. He had vaguely hoped it might. There were times, and this was one, when any clue to Kathy was welcome.

Dennis seemed to know his way around. He went through a door behind the bar and along a passage. Hugh followed reluctantly. He didn't want to stay nor did he much want to go back. Not yet.

The thought was worrying him that he would have to find another, non-private way to pluck Kathy out of her abysses, one he could employ in the presence of other people. The situation would inevitably recur, Kathy destroyed – she was so destructible, the initial breach having been born in her – and himself helpless because at the crucial moment he couldn't take her to bed. There had to be something to be going on with. Promissory perhaps? Help, if not at hand, manifestly on the way.

There was quite a pleasant garden behind the pub. A lawn sloped to pollard willows and a green river. Dennis carried his beer to the river bank and, setting the tankard on the grass, flung himself down.

It was typical of him to speak of sitting and then to lie at full length. Hugh thought of Kathy upright and unhappy in Cecile's garden a few miles away.

'She's very much in love with you. I expect you know,' said Dennis. 'You've discussed it?'

'Not in so many words.'

And not in those words, Hugh trusted. He preferred her cry – 'You don't like me!' – the useless little euphemism which could not obscure or safeguard what she felt. 'I intend to be good to her.'

'Will she be good to you?'

How did Dennis know that the question should be asked? Or that Hugh couldn't ask it and Kathy was too beset to frame it? Did he know that asking it was enough, was too much?

Flat on his back with his hands behind his neck he had the sun in his face. If he could see anything it could only be a Hugh-shaped mass. His eyes were like the solid eyes of a statue – the most solidly personal stare Hugh had ever sustained came from almost under his feet. 'That's my business.'

'Business' was an apposite word! Every minute of the day he had been busy with everything that had happened or might happen to her – and dreamed at night of all that hadn't happened and never could. He hadn't spared himself and now he was tired. Admitting it was a luxury, perhaps a treachery. It was so easy to betray her.

He had not looked at this garden and the trees and the river, he had only turned his eyes to them. He sometimes drove miles like that, and drove carefully, without seeing the road or anything on it, just seeing Kathy.

The question that had to be asked was self-answering. It was, after all, a fact, one he had always known. With an enormous reservoir of tiredness behind it. He hadn't seen Dennis either, except as an inkling of Kathy. But she was right, Dennis wasn't like her.

Dennis was gazing into the sun. He had forgotten Hugh or consigned him to the air which he breathed as lightly and evenly as if he were asleep. Hugh envied his stillness, he coveted the grass under him, the river and the shadows of the tree rocking him. He was very tired. He sat down, gingerly, and then, groaning, stretched himself on his back. Even his face was tired, he must have been frowning since the weekend began.

Dennis took his hand, not seizing hold but gently resting it in his and they lay side by side, the bones of Hugh's face relaxing one by one.

'You will be better off without me.'

It was true and usually they accepted it without thinking, but that morning at least two of them gave it thought. Her husband was one: he was slightly surprised and less slightly irritated to find himself thinking about it. He attributed it to the fact that being on holiday he had time to think about the unthinkable. It was, in its first and final analyses, unthinkable.

Simon, her eldest son, thought of his grandmother whom he had not liked and who had no more to say to console him when, at six years of age, he was about to go into hospital to have his tonsils out, than 'You'll be better off without them'. She too had had a screwy smile. He hoped his mother would not become like *her* mother.

The younger son, Matthew, said, 'I don't want to go.'

'What's that?' His father looked at him over the rim of his cup.

'Shark-fishing doesn't interest me.'

'You talked about nothing else before we left home.'

'That was then.'

'What's happened between now and then to make you lose interest?'

Matthew's light eyes opened wide in alarm. 'Nothing. Nothing's happened. I just ain't motivated.'

'Then you'd better get motivated. The boat's booked, the whole thing's been arranged for your benefit. And don't say *ain't*. Where on earth did you pick that up?'

'Everyone says *ain't*.'

'Not the people I know.'

'The people *he* knows,' said Simon, 'are all hayseeds and cowcakes.'

'It's settled. We're going and you're coming.'

'He wants to save sharks for posterity. He's into ecology. He spends hours at the boathouse watching worms.'

'Shut up!'

'It's your second home.'

'Both of you,' said their father, 'this is supposed to be a holiday.' Melissa, his wife, still smiled. She could be relied upon to have thought no farther than the operative word. In this case, 'holiday'. And in this case rightly, he conceded, she would stop there. He said to her, 'You must please yourself. We must all please ourselves.'

'Except me!' cried Matthew.

'You will please your father by going with him.' She touched Matthew and he recoiled. She flinched as if his hand had struck her instead of being snatched away. Ridiculous it was, and caused her husband renewed irritation. She could be relied upon to put her finger, manually and metaphorically, on the wrong place. She had touched the child who was going through some sort of crisis and just now could not bear to be touched, as she should know, she was his mother. Matthew, now, was scarlet in the face and ready for tears.

'Post hoc ergo propter hoc,' murmured Simon who was doing Latin and would probably go on quoting it for the rest of his life.

It was possible to dislike one's children at times. The times, for the father, were becoming less infrequent with their adolescence. He realised it was due to introspection based on surmise, an unproductive state of mind which he should have no time for. 'We leave at nine-thirty and return about four. Bring sweaters and wear your anoraks.' He went to the window. 'I hope this mist means heat.' He tapped sharply on the pane, but of course it was not a barometer and nothing happened. 'I shall go and get ready.'

His wife and sons sat on at the table. Simon finished the marmalade, Matthew stared glumly; Melissa, their mother, continued to smile.

'You got us into it,' Simon said to Matthew. 'Morning, noon and night it was "I want to go shark-fishing, can we go shark-fishing".'

'I've changed my mind, anyone can change their mind.'

'Last year it was can we go snorkelling, the year before that it was pony-trekking, the year before that it was can we make sandpies –'

'Go to hell.'

Simon glanced at his mother. She smiled, not at him, not, in fact, at anyone. Whether they were better off or not, they were definitely without her. He stood up, not unkindly knuckled his brother's head. 'Come on, kid, tempus fugit. Get your things.'

When they were alone Matthew said to his mother, 'What will you do?'

'I expect I'll go for a walk.'

'Where? Where will you go?'

'Perhaps I'll go and watch the swans.'

'You don't like the creek.'

'Don't I?'

'You said you didn't.'

'I don't remember.'

'You said it was sad!'

'It is, rather.'

'You won't go *there*?'

'I don't know.'

'You must know!' he cried, looking like his father. 'You must *know* you won't go there!'

'Is it important what I do?' She asked in all simplicity, without wryness, with something which Matthew, young as he was, knew to be innocence. He was suddenly unable to bear himself and jumped up from the table and ran out of the room.

His father, coming downstairs, said, 'Aren't you ready yet?'

Melissa watched from the window as they went through the garden. They did not turn to wave, and Matthew kicked the snapdragons.

It was quiet when they had gone, a supremely quiet house this, at the head of the deep, green creek. Even when they were all there the quietness could be felt. Intrusive. On Melissa it intruded, between unspoken thoughts and spoken words, her own and others'. And she had been conscious of it going on, for it was somehow a function, under all the sounds of living. She had once remarked in her husband's hearing how 'enormously quiet' the cottage was and he had said, 'Which is why we come here'. It might have been her reason, she thought now, feeling the pressure of the silence, for not coming.

In the window-glass where it was backed by a holly bush and reflective, she saw her face. It was smiling a left-over smile which strengthened as she quizzed it and thought that, like Queen Victoria, she was not amused.

While she washed the breakfast dishes and made the beds she pondered on the quality of this quiet. The function of silence. It could have several, and one would surely be the identification of noise. That, she smiled with real amusement and let the frypan fall into the sink, was a necessity. She listened to the dying of the clatter. It died fast, faster than in her kitchen at home. Or was it her imagination that the echoes were put down almost before they could begin to rise? There was perhaps a more sinister function – the destruction of noise, the phasing out of sound. Of life. Her small hairs crept on her neck. She felt, she always had, that this silence was hostile. She could feel it in every cranny of the house and it wasn't peace or quiet, it was a web, weaving.

She must be getting silly approaching her old age. Forty-eight was rapidly approaching it, in twelve years she would be sixty. A grand-mother perhaps. She did hope so. One's grandchildren were said to be more fun than one's own children, closer. It was something to do with being the second generation. She saw herself and someone very small, just reaching to her knee, going hand in hand through the house and garden. The quiet was evaporating before them. She saw herself identified. Certainly identification was needed. To the intrusive silence she said boldly, 'But not destruction!' and felt stronger for having spoken her mind. She saw herself, a grandmother, wiping egg from another baby's face.

She would go for a walk. Not to the creek, because Matthew did not want her to go there. She wished she could be sure why. Apparently because he thought it made her sad. But apparency was not always transparency with Matthew. He was growing up and often felt that he must be less than honest. It was a defence. She respected and did not try to break down the prickles with which he surrounded himself. She bled, at times, just the same. Someone had said to her once, 'I can't bear it when they start to grow up. They lose all their lovely little ways. They won't hold hands with you, they don't come and kiss you, they won't even look you in the face half the time. And they never tell you anything.' Melissa had been shocked. Not wanting one's children to grow up seemed to her wicked and selfish and perverse.

Whatever Matthew's reason, she would respect it and not go to the creek. Which left her the choice of a longer walk to the headland or a fraught one in the lanes which were so narrow in places that there was room for only one car, and pedestrians had to climb up the bank.

She decided on the headland. It would be a hot day, the mist was drying away, there would be no wind. Would it be good weather for shark-fishing? She hoped they wouldn't catch anything, that they would enjoy the trip and nothing would be killed.

Along the headland was a path that went up through gorse and thorn bushes, skirted fields of buttercups and scabious and dropped into bays where the seaweed was piled in ridges and the rocks endowed with moss like green chenille.

She looked for the boat that was taking her husband and children out to sea. She could not tell one boat from another. Matthew had tried to instruct her. 'That's a ketch, it's two-masted, and that's a sloop, it has only one mast – see? That's a corvette, there are her guns. That's a cabin-cruiser like we had at Weymouth, and that's a screw-steamer and that's –' 'Why is it a screw-steamer?' 'Because it's driven by a screw.' 'But I don't see how a screw –' she had wanted to understand, she might better remember if she understood – 'a screw that screws things together?' Matthew had been angry. He said, with bitter calm, 'Don't be an absolute idiot.' Later, he had told it as a tea-time story and they had all laughed, including herself. She would have liked the screw explained, but of course she could not ask again and had promptly forgotten what a screw-steamer looked like, and a ketch, and a sloop, to say nothing of a corvette.

Several boats were going out, she hoped they weren't all shark-fishers and she was, at the moment of hope, subjected to a vision of death throes. She saw a black creature thrashing the bloody water to foam, ribbons of pink flesh streaming from its side. She was prone to flashbacks of an inner eye, though they never flashed back to anything she could actually have seen, but were put together, she supposed, from dreams and fantasies, nightmares and childhood horrors. Illuminations, she supposed, of what might or might not be truth. Either way she could have done without them.

The boats were heading into the mist which had consolidated out at sea. The words of some poem came into her mind: 'Where are you going to, all you big steamers?' They weren't big, weren't even steamers; she waved a general wave to them. At once there was an answering movement from somewhere just below. She saw it without any certainty, it was anonymous and she was obliged to guess what had caused it. She guessed a bird's wing, a gull startled by her presence or a swan from the creek. Though answer it had seemed to. It came again and she saw why. It was a repetition of her wave, something white being moved to and fro down on the beach. Their beach. It was a strip of shingle and egg-shaped boulders leading directly to the creek and the boathouse. They kept it scavenged, rearranged the smaller boulders after the winter seas had piled them pell-mell, and Melissa had transplanted sea-pinks and scabious and rock-rose in the pockets along the cliff. Of course it wasn't really private and anyone had a right to be on it. Still, she was vexed that someone was, and was mimicking her. That's how it looked, but they might be trying to attract her attention. Might be needing help. She went down the path, unwillingly hastening her steps.

Rounding a bluff of rock she saw someone looking up at her. He was undoubtedly young, though he wore an elderly tweed hat. He had something white in his hand which he was now whirling round and round his head. When she came into view he stopped. She supposed he was staring at her, although she couldn't see his eyes under the brim of his hat. Then, slower and deliberately, he resumed the whirling, and kept it up while she negotiated the rest of the path, picking her way

[53]

instead of slithering down as she often did. From the very first moment she knew she had to be careful.

'Hullo,' he said, 'I thought you were someone else.'

'I'm sorry.' She need not have said that, she had nothing to be sorry for.

But he said, 'Oh that's all right,' taking it as an apology. 'I hoped you were my breakfast.'

When she said nothing he snatched off his hat with a gesture which was entirely disarming. Melissa, disarmed, saw that he was in his early teens, blond, dark-browed. He did not have the peeled-wand look which made Matthew, and sometimes Simon, look so vulnerable. His skin was dry and brown, the texture and colour of a free-range egg. She had to smile and he smiled too. His white teeth flashed. Oh, she thought, here's a charmer.

'It should have been here by now.' She raised her eyebrows. 'My breakfast!' He sounded so dismayed that again she had to smile.

'Do you have it on the beach?'

'Of course. I'm an eccentric.' He threw his hat back on his head experiencing, she plainly saw, delight in the idea – some of it at her expense. She would have liked to ask where his breakfast would come from since there were no houses near, apart from their own cottage. But she was wary of the explosive area under the skin of the very young. She couldn't avoid blundering into it in her sons, but with this boy there was no need. He was none of her business. 'It's not the same as being weirdo and freaking out. That's for show. It's real with me.' He thumped his stomach. 'Deep down I'm different. Hollow, I haven't eaten since yesterday tea-time.' Melissa turned away. 'I say, don't go. Please stay.' He brushed the sand off a slab of rock. 'Here's a seat for you.' It was in fact the place where she habitually sat on the beach. To one side was a little rock basin which the sea washed and replenished at each tide. 'Stay and talk.' He was pleading, she thought, surprised.

'I have things to do.'

'Oh please, just for a little while. At least until my breakfast comes.'

So she sat down, not too readily, and with a sense of guilt. Because if he hadn't pleaded she would have gone away, stiff-necked and deceitful, when she really wanted to stay.

How long was it since she had done anything without either having to stop and think whether she should do it, or to regret having done it? Who would trust anyone who could not trust herself?

'Of course I like being on my own, that's why I'm eccentric, I mean that's how I know I am. But I have to talk when I'm hungry.'

The rock basin was lined with sand. There were limpet shells in it and ribbons of green weed. 'Are you camping?'

'I'm not *that* eccentric.' He perched opposite her on a pinnacle of rock which could not have been comfortable. His jeans were tight to bursting at the knee and she had a totally unsought vision of the sharp rock piercing the tautly stretched cloth over his buttocks. 'I have a place of my own. A retreat.'

'You're staying here alone?' He nodded. 'Where are your parents?'

'In Nigeria, where my father's job is. Normally I'd have gone out for the hols, but there's a panic on and they thought I'd be in the way.'

'Panic?'

'Little black men putting on war-paint and beating tom-toms. Just letting off steam, really.'

'Who brings your breakfast?'

'The boy.'

'Boy?'

'We have houseboys, garden boys, kitchen boys, sweeper boys, pool boys. Mine's a general provider boy.'

'Is he black?'

'As your hat.' He opened wide his eyes which had been heavy, even sleepy, and his appearance was changed. Whatever he was seeing as he looked at her, to Melissa it was as if she was looking at his face for the first time. She was shocked without knowing why. 'Black wouldn't be right for you, you should wear crimson.' She heard the words but did not take their meaning. 'A big crimson hat with a feather under your chin.'

'I should look ridiculous.'

[55]

He had managed to put years on himself and it was in keeping with his sudden seniority that he did not contradict her. 'My name's Kimber. I intend to be a fashion designer. That's one of the things I intend to be. I haven't quite decided. I'm good at the other sort of figures, you see, and I could end up as a mathematician.'

The rock basin was rough, not completely round, and shallow. It reminded Melissa of the stone stoups for holy water in the walls of churches. When she dipped her fingers in she experienced a kind of blessing. 'Where is your house?'

'In Lagos.'

'I meant here.'

'You can just see the roof.' He gestured along the beach. 'I'll say this, it's handy for swimming, boating, diving and generally getting wet.'

'Isn't that the roof of Spur Cottage?'

'Yes, the Hardings' place. Mine's below it, by the creek. I know the Hardings.'

'You do?'

His voice warming, he leaned towards her. 'You could wear peacock-blue. Marvellous! Gros-grain or moiré, something stiff to contain you.'

'Because I'm shapeless?'

'No, fluid.'

Melissa did not much like the way the conversation was going. He obviously did. His eyes shone with percipient pleasure. She could not take exception to it. 'I don't care about clothes.'

'Ah but you should. Clothes speak for you. They tell everyone how you are. Don't you ever wonder why all the kids wear Levis and T-shirts?'

'Because they're comfortable?'

'That's only the half of it. It's so they'll look easy-going, to make it all look easy. Everything. Know what I mean? As if they don't have to try.'

She thought he might have a point. She was accustomed to, but still she dreaded, the expression of complete indifference she saw in her sons' faces. It could come so swiftly and inexplicably immediately after

– almost chasing off – any natural or logical expression of concern. She had thought it might be a blind, had hoped it was.

This boy wore jeans and a cricket shirt with sleeves rolled to his upper arms. His feet were bare. He smiled. 'Me, I don't want it easy.'

'What do my clothes tell you?'

'That you've forgotten who you are.'

'Really?'

'Yes, really,' he said sternly. 'I don't mean you've lost your memory, the ordinary part, you've lost the part that's yourself, the part that's you and nobody else. I *think* that's memory. A special sort.'

'You mean I've got no personality.'

'No I don't.' He cried fiercely, 'I mean you don't do yourself justice.'

'I don't know about justice but you're wrong about forgetting.' She had herself too much in mind, moments of forgetfulness came as a relief. Deliberately she stirred the sand at the bottom of the rock basin and they watched it smoke up into the clear water. 'I wish I could forget myself sometimes.' It sounded ridiculous when she had said it, full of pretence. Yet it was true, she longed to get away from the hoops which were just as shaming and pointless each time she was put through them.

He did not question her, she could not have borne it and certainly couldn't have answered if he had. He it was who apologised. 'Sorry, I'm talking crap.' He had a discretion beyond his years.

'Are you very hungry?'

'Starving.'

'I'll give you breakfast if you like.'

'Oh I'd like!' His joy pleased her even if it was only at the prospect of filling his stomach. 'I say, it's terribly kind of you.'

'Come along.'

'Where to?'

'I can't make breakfast here. We'll go to my house.'

'Where's that?'

It was her turn to gesture vaguely along the beach. She was smiling with something less than kindness as she moved away up the cliff path. It was only a very little less: a gentle relish at the thought of his face when she went into the gate of Spur Cottage.

But it didn't happen like that. Along the cliff path she stopped to look at some bright pink flowers. 'Do you know the name of these?'

He stooped and with his finger and thumb stroked the spikes of blossom. 'Sainfoin.' He looked up. 'I don't know yours.'

'Harding.'

'Harding?' He rose slowly to his feet. 'H-A-R-D-I-N-G?' Spelling it out his face was a picture, though not such a pleasure to her. Shock, consternation and dismay, none of it afforded her actual pleasure. His dismay went to her heart. 'You're Matthew's mother?' She nodded. 'He told me you were venerable!'

Suddenly his dismay, Matthew, herself – it was all wonderfully funny. She burst out laughing and he, seizing her hands, whirled her into a dance of delight. Together they went round and round among the sainfoin and the scabious.

Then she broke away, stood pinning up strands of hair which had fallen on her neck.

'That little creep!'

'Perhaps he just meant I should be venerated.'

'I say, I'm sorry, calling him that.'

'Why did you say your house is by the creek? There's only our cottage and the boathouse.' She pinned up the last strand of hair. 'That was a lie.'

'No.'

'I'm not complaining, you have every right to lie to me if it suits you. I just wondered why you should.'

'I didn't.' His brows darkened, drew together.

'Perhaps you don't know when you're lying. Perhaps it's just habit.' She was of course complaining, knowing all the time that she had no right to.

'I'm not a liar. And I'd never lie to you.'

'Why not?' He was scowling fiercely, almost comically, but her anger was bright and brittle. 'We're strangers. Surely it couldn't matter less what you say to me.'

'I *am* staying down at the creek. In the boathouse.'

'The boathouse!'

'Yes, if you must know.' He said wrathfully, 'You must, mustn't you. I've been there three days. Just to sleep. In the daytime I clear out to the beach or the headland so nobody knows I'm there.'

'Why are you there?'

'For a lark, really. I couldn't go to my parents for the holidays so they sent me to my uncle and aunt in Fulham. It wasn't much fun, they're out at work all day. I got fed up and hitched down here and I'm fending for myself.'

'But why in our boathouse?'

'It's better than a barn. I sleep in the old boat, it's got cushions and I found a blanket. I won't be any trouble.'

'Matthew knows you're here, doesn't he?' Matthew, she remembered, had not wanted her to go to the creek, had wanted to know that she definitely wouldn't go. It had mattered to him more than shark-fishing. 'Is he your friend?'

'Sort of. Of course he's much younger than me. I've been coaching him at cricket, he's very keen to play a good game.'

'He's the black boy who was to bring your breakfast?'

'It would have been just bread and marmalade. I bought biscuits and chocolate and Mattie brings me what he can. It isn't much, I mean it's not much to take, you wouldn't miss it. You're not meant to.'

Melissa smiled. 'I have thought we've been getting through a lot of bread lately. And a pint of milk I was counting on for a custard vanished from the kitchen table.'

'Sorry –'

'Why on earth didn't Matthew get us to invite you?'

'I turned up one day, he didn't know I was coming, he couldn't just produce me.'

'You can't go on sleeping in the boathouse. And hiding.'

'Why not? It's fun and I'm independent. I like the boathouse, when I'm in bed I can reach down and touch the water. Mattie joins me during the day whenever he can. And he needn't pinch any more food for me, I've got a little money.'

'The food doesn't matter, you must have enough to eat. But my husband wouldn't like you being here like this.'

'*You* wouldn't mind, would you?'

'That's not the point.'

'Mattie says his father doesn't like strangers.' She found his gaze disconcerting, she could see him putting two and two together. 'He says he doesn't like anybody much.'

Making three? Or five? 'That's not true.' She was alarmed. It was the sort of thing Matthew would say in one of his gloomy moods when he felt hard done by – by Fate rather than anyone in particular. It meant next to nothing, certainly not what she was putting into it. What was she putting into it? She thought that in a quite instinctual way she felt threatened. 'My husband is a busy man. He's brought work here with him and we try not to disturb him.'

'Like playing a nose-flute? Mattie got whacked for that.'

'Of course he didn't. He was punished not for playing the flute but for not stopping when he was told to.'

They had come to the last stretch of path before the cottage and he stood still. 'I shan't come any farther.'

'It's all right, they've gone fishing. That's why Matthew couldn't bring your breakfast.'

'He might have told me.'

'He didn't know he was going. My husband hired a boat and he's taken Matthew and Simon shark-fishing.'

'It'll scare the pants off Mattie.'

'It's something he wanted to do.'

'He sees trouble coming, things happening before they happen.'

So do I, thought Melissa, I see things happening that haven't happened, not to me, not yet. It's how I try to stop them. She hadn't known that Matthew protected himself that way too.

As they went up the garden path she said, 'Bacon, egg, fried bread – will that be all right?'

'It'll be great.' In the kitchen doorway he waited. 'Is there anything I can do to help?'

'Come in and sit down somewhere.' He bent to brush the sand off his bare feet. 'What shall I call you?'

'Kim for short. What shall I call you?'

'Mrs Harding.' He sat on a bar stool, his hands clasped between his knees, subdued, not meek – he would never be meek. How did she know that? What did she know about him? She even had some-thing to learn about her own son. 'What does Matthew see hap-pening?'

'Things like hitting his own wicket. Getting a ball in his eye. He'll never make a good batsman.'

'He's not a coward.'

'No, he's a good kid. Don't tell him you've seen me.'

'Why not?'

'Because that would be the end of it, I'd have to clear out. I don't want to, I like it here.'

She turned the bacon in the pan. 'It's a ridiculous situation.'

'I'm not doing any harm.'

'My husband wouldn't like it.'

'And he'd take it out on Mattie?'

'Of course not.'

'Mattie's scared of him.'

She had a vision of Matthew, the strings of his neck taut, his eyes wide but without candour, his lips tight and vengeful. She said again, 'Of course not,' out of loyalty to Matthew no less than to her husband, no less than to Simon, than to herself, to them all. She set the plate before him, saying firmly, 'You're quite wrong.'

'This looks terrific.' He cut up the bacon and bread and speared the pieces on his fork. He filled his mouth and beamed at her as he ate. 'It *is* terrific.'

'Have you brothers and sisters?' He shook his head. 'And you're separated from your parents. You can't know what it's like to be part of a family.'

[61]

Taking up the next forkful he said, without any great interest, 'What's it like?'

It was not the first time she had been called upon to explain what other people said without question. Yet she meant the same as they meant, at least she supposed she did, one had to suppose that. 'You can't put family feeling into words.'

He steered a piece of bread into the egg-yolk. 'Blood-ties don't count. I know plenty of people who can't stand their brothers and sisters or their mums and dads or their aunts, uncles and cousins. Or their granddads. Mattie's not the only one.'

'The only one what?'

He looked up from his food with the candour which Matthew had lost. 'The only one I wouldn't feel different about if he was my kid brother.' Surely, surely, she thought, in Matthew it was only a temporary loss, a passing phase, something to do with his age; it was always something to do with age, however young or old you were. 'It's not easy, being the headmaster's son. Some kids try to take advantage.'

'Advantage?'

'They expect me to fix things for them, get them off the hook. My trouble is I've got too many friends.'

'I thought your father worked in Nigeria.'

'So he does.' He smiled approvingly. 'They have schools there too. To teach the piccanins. My father speaks the native lingoes – Urdu, Ibo, Mulligatawny, Brown Windsor – the lot.'

'But you don't go to school in Nigeria?'

'Lord no. I wouldn't mind if I did. Their system's more democratic than ours.' She was aware that her question hadn't been answered and she couldn't ask it again, she wasn't sure what it was. He put his knife and fork tidily together on his plate. 'That was marvellous. The best breakfast I've ever had.'

'We're going home on Friday.'

'Friday! Mattie said you were staying till Sunday.'

'My husband has to be in London by the weekend.' As he gazed at her and she at him she felt his dismay reflected in her own face. 'What will you do?' How absurd she was being. His problems were of his own making and not for her to solve or even to sympathise with.

She picked up his plate and took it to the sink. He followed, stood behind her and touched – it was the lightest possible touch but she was sure he did – the nape of her neck. She swung round.

He was tall enough to look straight into her face, he was going to be a tall man and his bones had the tentative, collapsible look of rapid growing. His nose was big, well-fleshed and pure, and might in time become meaty. He laughed, his dismay had been only momentary. 'I'll eat seaweed and hitch home when my money runs out.'

She washed up his breakfast things, he found the tea-towel and dried them and she put everything away. She was being careful to leave no sign of his presence, perhaps she had already made up her mind to tell no one that she had seen him. Not even Matthew. Matthew least of all.

'It's a super day.' He opened the kitchen door. 'Let's go for a walk.'

'I have work to do.'

'What sort of work?'

'Housework.'

'You can do that any day. You're on holiday – do something you've never done before.'

'I've been for walks before.'

'Not with me.' He held out his hand. When she took it she realised they must look – for her, absurdly – like children running out to play – and she still had her kitchen apron on. Matthew had brought it back from his trip to Brittany, it had a picture of a soup ladle and the words 'Bon appetit!'

Why Matthew least of all? It must be because of the children running out to play, was it because she was competing with this boy on his own ground? She made him wait while she untied her apron and locked the door and then set foot, sedately, on the garden path.

The early mist had vanished. Between the last of the dew and the first real heat of the sun was a brilliance of line, a clarity which would be short-lived, for this was going to be another hot day, a trembler and a melter. During the drive down it had also been very hot and she had cried out in alarm that the road ahead went into a lake. Her husband had said that it was a mirage. Having thought, and still wishing to think, that a mirage was a green beautiful vision of life that came just before death in the desert, she had protested, 'But there are no palm trees.' Her husband said, 'Don't be a fool, Melissa.' Matthew burst out laughing and Simon explained that it was an optical illusion of a reflecting surface below eye-level, caused by the heat increasing the density of the air, and a whole lot more about the decreased velocity of light and wave-fronts and refractions and displaced images until his father ordered him, for God's and all their sakes, to shut up.

Melissa, looking out to sea, saw that the boats were melting away. The line between sea and sky was the first to go and already it had gone. When she turned to look inland she saw – it would probably be for the last time that day – the diamond flash of a water drop hanging on a thorn. She thought of Simon and his refracted light.

'I shan't call you Mrs Harding.' The boy, Kim, danced backwards before her. His bare feet plunged among the tussocks of grass and razor-sharp dried mud and small fierce thistles that grew low in the turf.

'Why not?'

'It's someone else's name, not yours.'

'Where are your shoes?'

'At the boathouse. Missuses are non-persons.'

'Go and put your shoes on. You could cut yourself on broken glass, or wire. Please,' she said, 'It hurts me to see you –'

He turned, and ignoring the path, broke his way down the hillside. Melissa shuddered, seeing his naked feet impaled on thorns, his small bones caught and cracked by the iron roots of gorse.

She sat on the grass to wait. She would not tell him her name. Without wishing to be a non-person she preferred not to be known as the Melissa whom her children knew, on the authority of their father, to be a fool, and for whom God and her family were called upon to suffer. She would have liked to start with a clean slate. It wasn't possible. She had become a pointless person. Frequently now she felt her acts and intentions to be without any real point. She no longer knew what the real point was, only what was to be gained by having it – a kind of belonging. She was often alarmed by her alienation. There were times when she felt as out of place as a sore thumb and the soreness, the hurt, seemed to be the symptom of a secret sickness – which was sensed by those about her and must soon begin to show.

The boats now were poised in mid-air. She could see the sky under them. In a court of law – it was one of her husband's worries, 'What would they do with you in a court of law?' – she would swear she had seen the sky under the hulls.

The boy, Kim, came along the path, running, his shoes in his hand. 'I wasn't long, was I? I didn't wait to put them on.' He threw himself down beside her and she caught a whiff of something not yet stale, not quite sweat, a kind of bodily ardour which she had noticed coming off the skins of her own sons. 'I was afraid you'd get fed up and go.' So, she was thinking, he wasn't sure about *me*. 'Let's go to Gunhallow, there's something I want to show you.'

'There's only a church at Gunhallow.'

'It's in the church, what I want to show you.'

He took her hand and drew her to her feet. They were standing together and his joy, which was reasonable perhaps because it did not reason, matched her own which was not. 'Come on!'

'I don't run everywhere, like you.'

He laughed. Then he said soberly, 'I couldn't have gone into the church with bare feet,' and dropped her hand and motioned her to go ahead of him along the path. So they walked to Gunhallow, Melissa's skirt brushing the ragwort and campion and where the gorse bushes met over the path he stepped in front and held them back for her. He did not speak and nor did she, and as the bushes leaned ever deeper into the path he circled round her, lifting aside the yellow spikes of gorse with a gallant gesture which she acknowledged with an inclination of her head, furling and unfurling her skirt as she passed the clutching brambles. She felt as if she were moving to some unheard stately measure and the thought must have struck them both because they smiled at each other and without a word made a deliberate solemn dance of it. Melissa didn't worry about how she looked or what people would think if they saw her. She who had to remember to try not to look foolish, so far forgot herself as to believe she was leading a dance – she who could never dance, had been told she lacked a sense of rhythm. 'It's just a matter of co-ordination,' she had been told at dancing-class; and later, her first boyfriend, angry and impatient, had declared, 'You've got two left feet!' She moved, now, expertly over the rough ground, she found that she *was* expert at such simple, gracious movements. They took shape in herself, instinctive, and she could not go wrong. She had the golden confidence which came to her blessedly but briefly after one small sherry. She might even be a little drunk on the sweet coconut smell of the gorse. It was as consequential as a dream sequence: she, an all but middle-aged woman and this boy, this child, twirling, treading and formally acknowledging each other among the brambles and the dried mud-prints of cattle.

They met no one and, when the path turned inland towards Gunhallow, by unspoken mutual consent continued their dance across the meadow, through buttercups and cow-parsley and wild garlic. The church came into view, she saw it as she sank into one of her almost curtseys. The clock started to strike. They both stood still.

'This is when Cinderella ran home,' said Kim.

'It won't strike twelve, not even twelve noon.' He snatched off one of his shoes, threw it into the air, caught it, threw it again and was fully absorbed, away from her, in a game. She cried, 'I hate that story!'

'Why?'

'Those glass slippers must have been hideously uncomfortable. And she had to dance in them for hours.'

'So she must have been glad when she could shake them off and run home.'

'Those poor Ugly Sisters, cutting off their toes and heels to get the slipper on –' She saw, as she had always been able to see, the chopped stumps forced into the glass and blood filling it, brimming over – 'it's a horrible story.'

He caught his shoe and came to her with it in his hand. 'They wouldn't do it, you know. Women are fussy about their feet.'

'Promise me, if you become a fashion designer you'll never design glass shoes.'

'I promise.'

Gunhallow church was old and so sunken that it was doubtful if even the last Trump would summon it out of itself. The ivy, which had probably split the tower in the first place, was now holding it together. The clock stirred and whirred inside like a flock of birds.

'I was here yesterday,' he said, opening the lych-gate. 'That's how I know.'

'Know what?'

'You'll see.'

They went between gravestones covered with moss and lichen which ranged from cabbage yellow to peacock green. The slabs, too, had sunk, some tipped this way, some that, a noseless angel lay back on her wings and a stone galleon foundered in a sea of dandelions. The general effect was casual and cheerful – like a room after a party.

But there had been no party in the church. It was a dark rough place, the pillars of the nave were of blackish stone, the roof beams of blackish wood, closely latched, with little generosity about them. They did not encourage the eye upwards, Melissa thought they were like the ribs of a lobster pot. She seemed to have brought the party spirit in with her and couldn't be reverent or even respectful.

She tripped over a hassock which had been left in the aisle and cried 'Damn!' before she could stop herself.

Kim caught her arm to steady her. 'Look.'

'Look where?'

He pointed. 'There. Do you see yourself?'

What she saw was a brightness, a vigour of colour unwonted in that dark place, there was a great shine, a glisten without substance or coherence.

'Myself?' Moving closer, staring for all she was worth, she made out the shape on the wall. It was a ship's figure-head, gaudily painted, highly varnished, the head, shoulders, arms and bosom of a woman. It fairly spanked out of the gloom, the last thing she would have expected to see, belonging, as it did, to the sea and to sailors.

'She came from a ship called the *Belle-Amie* which went aground on Gunhallow Ledge two hundred years ago. Next month will be the anniversary of the wreck and they've painted her ready for the ceremony.' Of course this church belonged to the sea, it had been built to be the last bit of good men saw when they sailed away and when they drowned. 'I think she looks like you.'

'Like me!' That great glistening face surrounded with dollops of black hair, cherry lips curved in a simper, eyes as big as boiled eggs and coloured a staring navy blue – she could have been annoyed, that at least would have been dignified. She couldn't admit, let alone cope with, the dismay that filled her. She was ready to weep, and it would have been all the same, no better, no worse, if the creature had been naked to the waist as so many of these old figure-heads were. Mercifully she was respectably though precariously covered, her robe caught and held on the points of her mammoth nipples.

Kim climbed on one of the pews beneath the figure. He turned to smile at Melissa. 'Isn't she beautiful,' and his fingers moved lightly, innocently – anything other than innocence could only be in her mind – down the wooden neck and stroked the wooden bosom. 'I shall call you my Belle-Amie.'

'You will call me Mrs Harding.'

When his face clouded and he said, 'It means beautiful friend,' she cried, 'I know what it means but that thing isn't beautiful and nor am I!'

He stepped down from the pew and, with the dignity she should have shown, said, 'I think you are.'

She shivered. 'It's cold in here.' The chill, the frisson, had nothing to do with temperature, it was a warning. She turned and hurried away between the aisles, again tripping over the hassock. No dignity, no self-respect, she was low on self-respect just now. Outside the church she said she must go back to the cottage, she had a lot to do, shopping, cooking, and the rest.

'Come with me to the cove. It's not far. Oh please!'

She had intended to spend at least part of the day pleasing herself, it was surely no fault or business of hers if doing so also pleased this boy. He was, if not accidental, entirely unforeseen, and why should she deprive herself of a walk, or of anything, because of him? Surely the way to reinstate herself in her own estimation, such as it was, was to almost disregard him. Politeness need be all: for her it had better be.

She took the way they had come across the field and when she reached the cliff top made for Gunhallow Cove, walking as if she were alone, and wished to be. When he spoke she turned her head or threw up her hand and went on listening to her feet among the grasses. She heard him behind her, their two pairs of feet clicked through the dry grass stalks with the tiny metal sound of high summer.

As they went down the path to the cove she slipped and would have fallen had he not caught her. She pulled away with a gesture which she immediately regretted but could not retract.

'Are you angry because I said you were beautiful?'

She was not sure whether he spoke as a child, artlessly, or as a man, ruthlessly. 'Of course not.' It was a long time since anyone had told her she was beautiful. Not since she was a girl, and even all those years ago, even then it had struck her as unlikely and she had giggled. To this minute she remembered the anger of the man, not her husband, who perhaps had had the words wrung out of him and was feeling a fool speaking them. After that she had been careful, but no one else had said it since. 'Flattery will get you nowhere.'

'I don't say what I don't mean.'

She went down the beach, looking for the boats. They had quite gone into the haze. It was not an omen, certainly it was no excuse, for her husband and sons would expect, and had every right to, that while they were away she would keep the character they had assigned her. She was not altogether happy with it, but what else, who else did she want to be? The question, her husband would have said, was academic – if he considered it a question. How could he, without knowing the extent of her misgivings?

She looked about her for somewhere to sit. Kim took off his hat and dusted a rock with it. She leaned against a slab, driving her heels into the sand for purchase. She said coldly, 'You know you can't stay.' His face and neck had reddened as if with sunburn. She saw the scarlet 'V' at his throat and in her mind's eye the white, minimal, male child's breasts under his shirt. 'My husband will lock up the boathouse when we go, he locks everything up.'

'But you won't tell him about me – you won't tell anyone?' He was pleading again, and drawing down his brows, scowling at her; she knew all about the pleading-bullying, her sons employed it to get their own way.

'What about Matthew? How can I pretend to him that I don't know?'

'You don't have to, just don't say anything. Mattie won't twig.' He tipped his hat to the back of his head, then laid his finger across his lips and winked. 'It ain't so difficult.'

Everyone said *ain't*. Matthew saw and accepted the world in this boy. 'I daresay we could fit you in somewhere.'

'I don't want to be fitted in. I want to be on my own. I want to be free.'

'Oh, free.' It was nothing she wanted to be. She needed to belong, to be an integral part, however small. Freedom, being alone, would have been terrifying. She pushed her feet deeper into the sand, it ran over her instep and trickled into her shoes.

Kim sauntered along the beach. He stooped among the rocks, dipped into pools. He picked up a knout of seaweed and whirled it round his head.

What did she think she was a part of? Perhaps *that* was the question. I am part of a family unit, she said to herself. And not such a small part either, she thought, because as well as providing the food for the family, and its creature comforts, she had provided the family.

That made her smile. She felt she had the best of the world – she had her family connection and the salt sun on her face, sand in her shoes, her husband and sons sailing peacefully with a margin of sky under their boat – and now this boy on the beach.

He came back to her, bringing the seaweed, ribbons of it hanging from a single stalk, glistening green and amber, frilled and dimpled and thick as a motor tyre. When she touched it it was glassy-smooth, cold, and cleanliness itself. The grains of sand did not sully it. She was overwhelmed by intense longing for absolutely nothing she could think of.

'Look,' said Kim, holding out his hand.

'What is it?' Being short-sighted she had to stoop and peer. There were tiny shells on his palm, just about the daintiest creations she had ever seen. Perfect copies of conch and whelk, winkle and cowrie shells. Some were minute turrets, twisted and furled, colours not of the rainbow but of buttercups and peach pearl, tender pink, purple streaked and russet brown. She held them up one by one. 'They're lovely.'

'And Belle-Amie isn't?'

'I prefer these.'

How full of light his eyes were, she felt she was being illumined. She might have gone so far as to feel glorified, but she couldn't allow that.

'There's something else I want to show you. It's part of the same thing really.'

'I don't want to see any of that again.'

'It's the *Belle-Amie* – the ship itself.'

'You said it was wrecked.'

'It was. Sometimes you can see it on Gunhallow Ledge. Not always, because it's terribly deep and the tide has to be on the turn and no wind. Wind makes white water and brings weed and stirs up the sand. It has to be right, like today, like now. Now will be right. You must come.'

'Where to?'

'Over there, by the rocks. That's where I was standing yesterday when I saw it, the whole thing, stem to stern. Don't you believe me?' She neither believed nor disbelieved, she was reluctant because to think of the ship was to think of that horrendous figure-head. 'It's something to do with the light. The image is bounced from one layer to another, like sound waves.'

'You mean it's an optical illusion.'

'No I don't. It's real and I was allowed to see it. You'll be allowed too.'

There were no two ways about it. In his brilliant gaze she was glorified and it had everything to do with the light.

They went down to the slabs that had split from the land and fallen as a rough causeway across the beach. The sea covered them exceptionally, in storms and winter tides, and the rocks now were warm to the touch. Touching them, Melissa was buoyed up by warmth.

'You stand here,' said Kim, 'and look right down and when there's a skin on the water you'll see it.'

'A skin?'

'Wrinkles. When you see the water wrinkling.'

The sea at the end of the causeway was smooth and guava green. She thought, I have to do some shopping. 'I can't see anything.'

'It's been there for two hundred years!'

She took the rebuke, which surely was that she mustn't expect to see the thing so soon. She stooped, then knelt on the rock. There was something about him, over and above being a child, which made humouring him important. We need bread, she was thinking, and eggs and supper for tonight. Sausages perhaps, and French-fries; sausages would travel – as far as the boathouse, anyway. Had she been asked what she was expecting to see she would have said nothing. Yet part of her mind, that part which supplied the visions, was preparing to see a fully-rigged ship, sails, pennants and all, under the water. It was the kind of foolishness she was known for. Her husband, a short-suffering man, declared that she didn't think. It was partially true, for she thought either too late or too soon. Relevance was what she lacked, her husband said.

She saw a streak on the water, a thread, no more than a cotton really.

'There!' He fell to his knees beside her. 'Look!'

She was never sure what it had amounted to. All she remembered afterwards was a brown shadow with edges that seemed to smoke. She cried, 'I see it!' and of course it was how it would look after two hundred years under the sea. More threads appeared on the water, a positive skin, and she leaned down. The shadow dissolved.

'You can see it?' Kim bent over her, holding her shoulders. 'Where?'

'It's gone.'

'You saw the *Belle-Amie*?' He pulled her round to face him. 'What did you see?'

'It was down there. The sand must have shifted and covered it. It was long and brown.'

He held her facing him, knee to knee, his smile breaking out. 'What did it look like?'

'Like a shadow.' No sails, no pennants. She was thinking now, and surely at the right time? 'A long narrow shadow – like an ironing-board.'

'A what?'

'It would be, wouldn't it, after two hundred years –'

He shouted with laughter and fell about with the same boisterous clowning as her sons did, and she was in the same vacuum, a figure of public fun.

'It's not there, is it?' she said. 'It never was. You're making a fool of me,' and climbed to her feet. Her knees were stiff, the sun hadn't softened the rock. The sun wasn't warm. The warmth was illusion, something to do with the light.

She crossed the slabs to the beach. The boy came running and ran backwards before her with his hat in his hands. He said, 'A fool?', as he had said, 'A what?', but he was not laughing. 'I wasn't going to tell anyone I'd seen it. Not even Mattie. It was going to be my secret. I don't know if anyone else has seen it, I think it moves about and it'll break up on the rocks and no one will see it ever anyway.'

She didn't personally think that would be any great loss. 'There'll still be the figure-head in the church.'

'Then I met you and I wanted you to see it. I wanted to share it with you.'

'Why?'

'Because there's nothing else I can.' He was at the midway age and could be a child one minute and man the next. She wondered if he consciously made the switch or was it done by inner workings over which he had no control? In any event, he was the man now, experiencing a man's emotions – towards herself, if you please. She did not please. Her husband and sons had every right to expect her to be sensible, mature and motherly and she clung to the image though she could not live, and keep living, up to it. 'Except me being here. It would be our secret if you didn't tell them.'

'You're a secretive person.'

'When it matters.'

'Matthew knows you're here, share the secret with him.'

'It's not the same.'

The way he looked at her, people would say was knowing, and perhaps she should say so too. 'I must go, the shops shut at one.'

'Will you come and talk to me? It gets lonely in the evenings.'

'You have Matthew.'

'Come to the boathouse and talk to me when they're all in bed.'

'What about my husband?'

'Doesn't he go to bed?'

'He expects me to go with him.'

A curious thing happened. The child and man coincided in his face, for a moment they both looked at her with their different angers: the child's murderous, the man's despising.

'I bent over backwards to please them,' said her husband. He lit a cigarette, a sure indication, if any was needed, that he was put out. The fact that it was needed did not ensure that it was observed. She hadn't yet realised that he had given up smoking. She still put out ashtrays, dusted and even washed them in the washing-up water after the dishes were done. 'Simon was reluctant to get his hands dirty and Matthew whined.'

'Didn't you enjoy it?'

'I'm getting too old for that sort of thing. At their age I would have given not just my eye-teeth but every tooth in my head to go shark-fishing. I had to be satisfied with sticklebacks.'

'Were they disappointed at not catching anything?'

'I think if we had they'd have thrown up or fainted. What did you do with yourself?'

'Walked to Gunhallow.' She seemed about to say something more, then looked at him with a kind of obduracy. 'Afterwards I went into Tredinnick shopping.'

'And stocked up with sausages.'

'The boys like them.'

'So do I, but not to the exclusion of all else.'

'I thought –' it was apparent that she had not – 'you and I might have eggs.'

He sighed. 'Am I to believe that two boys can consume five pounds of sausages in two days?'

'Three –'

'Mel,' he pulled deeply at his cigarette, 'I counted five packs in the fridge.'

'It would be nice to take some home. They're so much better than we get in London.'

'That's different, that's sensible. I'm all for taking them home. And I should enjoy some for my supper tonight. Just tonight, not tomorrow for breakfast, nor lunch, nor made into burgers to eat on the journey.'

'The boys –'

'Can have what they like, sausages at every meal if they like. I no longer know what my children like.'

She went and stood behind him, gently, easingly moved her fingers into the muscles at the back of his neck. He groaned and leaned his head against her. 'Sticklebacks and a smell of whale was all I got when I was a kid.'

'Whale?'

'In Dreamland, the funfair, amusement park, whatever they call it now, at Margate. There was a whale on show, degutted and soaked in formalin. It stank to high heaven. Outlandish. It drove us wild.' He sighed. 'We got more romance out of that stink than our two out of their shark-fishing – which, incidentally, cost a packet.'

'Although you didn't catch anything?'

'My dear girl, it's not on a sale-or-return basis.'

'I thought they might make a reduction —'

'Is the manatee still in Gunhallow church?'

'The what?'

He sat forward and gingerly turned his head on his neck. 'Ah, that's better. The wooden mermaid. A manatee is a sea mammal, supposed by some to be the original mermaiden. Rather an ugly brute by all accounts. So is that thing in the church.'

'Yes, it's still there.'

'Quite out of place. Heathen, in fact. The sailors thought figure-heads would frighten off the sea-devils. They kept the Bible for Sundays. Had to hedge their bets in those days.' He stood up, stretching and luxuriating. 'You've the touch, Mel. Let's have a drink, eat, and go early to bed.'

Melissa did not wait until he was asleep, she was not waiting or purposing, she was hardly thinking. She went to bed and lay curled, as she always did, on her right side, her arms about herself, not for warmth or comfort but so as not to disturb her husband who wakened at a touch and was often unable to get to sleep again. She had made no conscious decision to stay awake, she lay docilely watching the granules of dark form and reform, and listening to his deep breathing. She felt no responsibility, yet was aware of an element of danger which seemed to have been devised specially for her.

Presently she gingerly raised the sheet and crept from under it. She dressed in the dark, knowing that it might be for nothing because Matthew could have had the same thought – Matthew, strenuously staring round the table at supper, defying anyone to notice when he transferred slices of bread and a sausage to his lap. She had hoped he had had the foresight to put the bread first and the sausage on top. How absurd they were being – and she so much the more absurd!

Matthew was looking after his friend, but she – unable to find the belt of her dress in the dark she took her husband's tie and knotted it round her waist – she was deceiving her husband. He would not approve of the boy hiding in the boathouse. There would be the

[76]

principle of it, and something else: he would resent her part in it, the little he could know he would resent without surprise. It was the sort of silliness he expected of her. But there was the other silliness which he would not expect. And nor would she.

On her way downstairs she looked into Matthew's room. He was sound asleep. But it was too late, she had visualised the encounter, both of them on the same errand, his rage and resentment at her sharing his secret as fiery as his father's was cold. She felt as diminished as if it had happened.

Then, by the light of the moon, shining on this side of the house, she saw the bread and sausage on the table by his bed. She saw too that he was not undressed, still in his shirt and trousers. It was obvious what had happened. He had lain down to await the moment to take Kim his supper and had fallen asleep. He wouldn't wake until morning. Kim had had no supper and perhaps no lunch. It was her responsibility. Because she had chosen to hide him she was immorally bound to feed him.

She went to the kitchen, put bread and butter, sausages, apples and cake on plates, put the plates in her shopping basket and covered them with a napkin.

There was no light in the boathouse. Perhaps he was asleep, or trying to be. And hungry, boys of his age were always hungry. She knocked on the window, called 'Kim, it's me.'

He was suddenly behind her, crying, 'It's you!' so loudly and joyfully that she put her hand over his mouth.

It was a long time since she had been in the boathouse. When he switched on the light she saw the paraphernalia, the – to her – useless and unusable things to do with boats and fishing, some of them so remotely she couldn't see the connection. Like the old Spong mincing-machine that had once been in the kitchen at the cottage and was now clamped to the workbench among a welter of tar-pots, rusty nails, yoghurt cups, rope-ends, hooks and cigarette stubs which must have been there since the summer before last when her husband had given up smoking.

'Are you hungry?'

'I was. I went into Tredinnick and got some fish and chips with my last fifty pee.'

'Matthew meant to come but he fell asleep waiting.'

'It's OK. He said he'd bring sausages and I hate the things.'

'Oh – I thought –' He was gazing at her, certain that she would have thought something, and waiting to hear. She took out the apples and cake and left the bread and sausages in the basket. 'I thought you might like this.'

'Apples! That's great, what I need. Mattie brings white bread and cold bacon. I said to him, where's the fibre? He said, "It's my breakfast, if I don't eat it I can do what I like with it", and I said, "Man, I mean vegetable, not moral." '

'He doesn't like brown bread.'

'Dundee cake! How did you know it's my favourite?'

'It's bought, I'm afraid. I can't make cakes.'

He nodded. 'Mattie said,' and took a bite.

She wondered what Matthew had said. 'Man, she even burns the toast.' Perhaps he had not said anything of the kind. He had a far-reaching pride, sometimes he wouldn't speak or hear spoken a word against the people or things he was connected with. She had heard him maintain, against all evidence to the contrary, that there was nothing wrong with his old clapped-out bicycle and indignantly refuse to have any repairs. Might she hope, at least, that he felt the same loyalty towards her?

'I've got something to show you.'

She said, smiling, 'What is it this time? Another mermaid?'

'What?'

'That thing in the church.'

One moment he was a boy with his cheek full of cake. The next, his face lengthened, lost its identity and he became ageless. She felt rebuked. 'You can't be very comfortable here, no bed, nowhere to sit.'

'I've got the boat. I lie in it with the doors open and watch the sunrise. I expect you think that's crappy.'

'No. I think –' again he waited to hear what she had thought – 'I would do the same.'

'Here's what I want to show you.' From the locker under the seat of the boat he brought out a length of cloth, jade green and heavy textured. She had seen it before, in Matthew's room at the cottage. 'It's one of the old dyes, made from roots or wood, before they used chemicals. They used to take ages, grinding and pulping and fermenting.' He shook out the cloth, it was creased and had obviously been serving as a blanket. 'It's your colour. I can see you in it. Draped and falling straight to the ankle. Like this.' He hung it from his shoulder, held it to his thighs with one hand chastely placed. 'This would be the general effect, but of course on me it looks comic.'

'So it would on me.'

'You'd have to let down your hair.'

'You want me to look like that figure-head.'

'I don't!' His vehemence surprised her. 'That's just a bit of wood, varnished and painted and stood up for holy.'

'Not my style.'

He drew a deep breath. 'You –'

She said quickly, 'I know what I am.'

'Mattie's mother?' She nodded. 'And the rest,' he said soberly, took off the blanket and folded it against his chest. 'You see, I know what you could be.'

It was too much. He needed a firm hand. Like her husband's. Her husband's hand would put him in his place as it put Matthew and Simon in theirs and would continue to do so until the imprecise moment when they moved to another place and became men. She picked up her basket. 'I must go back.'

'I'm going for a swim. I love swimming at night, don't you?'

'I've never tried it.'

'Really? The water's like silk.' He threw the blanket into the boat. 'Come with me now, let's go and swim.'

'You go if you want to.'

'Come and watch me.'

'It's dark –'

'There's a full moon, you can see for miles.' He pushed open the doors of the boathouse. The sea was as he had said, like silk, live and scandalously rich. The scandal was how such beauty could be achieved without thought. She was going to marvel at it and never forget the sight, it was going to be behind this holiday, this episode. But there was a snub somewhere. Not just to her, to the whole world, to everyone except this boy who turned to her crying, 'Look! Isn't it the most fantastic!'

She followed him to the beach. Why she followed she could not have said. Mrs Melissa Harding, approaching fifty, satisfactorily married to a man who still expected – demanded – satisfaction, with two growing sons and an enviable home – 'I do envy you your house,' more than one woman had said – simply could not bear to be parted from a schoolboy. Certainly not by the sea. She looked at it with hatred: live silk, thousands of miles wide, exquisitely concealing – denying – unspeakable depths, monsters, drowned men, rotting slimy things.

Kim ran to the rocks, threw off his clothes, stood naked, arms spread wide, drew them together in one swift compass movement, and dived.

From where she stood she did not see him enter the water. She saw jaws open and him going down the gullet of the sea. She saw herself helplessly running to and fro, mewing, and Matthew's fury and her husband's cold disgust. She also had a glimpse, no more than a blink, a shutter opening on a brilliant scene, of a body, lifeless, swollen and twined with weed.

Then his head appeared, he struck out from the shore and she stood watching the brown cork of head bobbing, nearly negligible after all, and started by asking herself a question, one of the many she should have asked already, and provided valid or at any rate presentable answers. Here she was, standing watching like a mother, like all the mothers who watched from this beach. But it was night and the child was not hers. So what was she doing?

When he turned and swam back to the rocks she knew that she was waiting. It was neither a valid nor presentable answer, she was alerted, nerves, muscle, her whole cage of bones tensed as if for a blow. And something else, no illusion. She was made aware of the hardening of her breasts under her dress. Oh God, he's only a boy, she thought wildly. That might well be why. For though she had looked on her own sons' boyhood a thousand times, this boy's perfection owed nothing to her. It was not of her flesh and therefore suspect.

But that was only a small part of the why. The rest, all the rest, she had been avoiding from the beginning. The beginning of what?

Kim stood up, came out of the sea, a white child, not silver or ivory or human, a piece of modern technology – plastic probably, and some kind of mercy was allowed her. Shivering, she bowed her head.

He came and stood beside her. 'I say – you're cold!'

'No –'

He grasped her hands and held them to the rock. 'Feel how warm it still is from the sun.'

She pulled herself free. 'I must go.'

'Wait till I get my clothes.'

She might have got away, fled back to the cottage and her sleeping family, it would have been an acceptable retreat. But she stood while he bounded away down the beach. Nothing she did now would be presentable ever again.

He hauled on his trousers and ran back to her, arms upheld, his shirt slung between, clinging to his wet skin. She helped him pull it free. His flesh was warm to the touch, breathed warmth before she touched it, her own was cold and stiff. She fancied she heard a rustle and whisper as she opened her mouth to speak, like the noises inside the old clock at Gunhallow. 'You should have brought a towel.'

'Haven't got one.'

'Oh – I'm so sorry –' conscience-struck, she thought of other necessities he could be lacking. 'How do you manage –'

'To dry myself? I roll on the grass. Let's sit down, I don't feel like going to bed yet.'

'I can't stay.'

'Will you come tomorrow?'

'I doubt it. I shall be packing. We leave early on Friday morning.'

He took an apple from her basket and broke it in half with a turn of his wrists. 'I'll always be glad I learned to do that. It impresses people no end. Yet it's really quite easy, just a matter of co-ordination.'

'Like dancing.'

He gave her half the apple and bit into the other. 'You could stay.'

'I can't. My husband will wonder where I am.'

'Stay on, after Friday I mean.'

'After Friday?'

'Not them. Just you. Over the weekend.'

'It's out of the question!'

'Why?'

She had a crazy thought about the half apple being symbolical. Of half what? Here she was, wholly and unutterably tempted. 'I couldn't possibly! There's too much to do at home.'

'Like what?'

'Like cooking and washing and ironing and mending. Simon goes back to school, and Matthew –'

'Not for another week. Let them fend for themselves for once. Mattie can make scrambled eggs and he says Simon's hardly ever in.'

'What about my poor husband? He hates scrambled egg.' Her husband's poverty should have made her smile, for he was a provident man and lacked nothing, except an adequate wife. She looked at the boy with dismay, it was an old dismay but had become and was becoming ever deeper. 'Why do you want me to stay?' That, of course, was obvious, so that he could move into the house and be comfortable. This time she smiled, wryly.

'We could have such a marvellous time.'

'Doing what?'

'We could talk, that's one thing we could do.'

'Talk?' Even that one thing she was obliged to mistrust. 'What about?'

'Everything!' Seawater trickled down his cheek and he dashed it away, impatient with her rather than with his wet hair. 'Mattie's only a kid, all he wants to talk about is football and sex.'

'Sex?'

'He's into it – didn't you know? A bit early.' He smiled with devastating sweetness. 'It's not as if he can *do* anything.'

Devastated, she cried, 'Of course I can't stay!'

He shrugged, then let his shoulders droop. 'It wasn't true about the *Belle-Amie*. Not literally. I made it up.'

'Why?'

'To get you interested.'

When almost anything would have done, she thought, or nothing, and laughed before she could stop herself. 'The figure-head's real enough.'

'Oh that. It came off some old tub sometime or other.'

'And there's no *Belle-Amie*?'

He looked at her through a drop of seawater clinging to the lashes of one eye. 'Yes. There's you.'

'I'm sure you can manage without me.'

'Perhaps we can,' said her husband. 'My concern is not what we shall do without you but what you will do without us. Alone here.'

'I shan't do anything. Just relax.'

'I didn't realise you were over-worked, over-committed.'

'I'm not, it isn't that at all –' Irony was wasted on her, how could one feel guilty when one never knew what would upset her? To take an extreme analogy, it was like walking in a minefield. 'I just like being here,' she said. He had, however, felt guilty, and forebore to ask why, when they had been coming here for years, she suddenly loved the place so much that she could not bear to leave. 'It's silly, I know –'

'It's unusual. It's unlike you.'

Then she said something which *was* silly, and with an earnestness which was even sillier, and tiresome. 'What am I like?'

[83]

'My dear, you must do as you please.' He went to the window, fretfully tapped the glass, disregarding the fact that it was not a barometer. 'The weather is going to change. If you really mean to stay on I must ask you to be very careful about locking up and making sure that all windows are closed when you leave on Monday. You will have to turn the water off, and the fridge – which must of course be emptied of perishable food – and bring all the keys with you. And ring in good time for a taxi to Penzance. You see, there's a lot to be thought of.'

'I'll remember everything.'

He doubted that. 'Take the early train on Monday otherwise I shall run into the homebound traffic when I come to meet you.' He added triumphantly, for it did seem to clinch the matter, 'You don't like being alone at night!'

She couldn't deny it. She lowered her head and stretched her neck, like a small inexperienced bull – as he might have told her, since she had just asked, but it would serve no useful purpose. He recognised the streak of obstinacy which she displayed, usually over trivia or, as on this occasion, something quite out of keeping and beyond his comprehension.

Melissa, who knew how unreasonable it must look, was wishing the moment over. It was, would eventually become, a minor incident to her husband. He would forget it, except as an instance of the way, the several ways, in which she failed to give satisfaction. There were women, she knew, who would have been able to give it, even in this situation, who would have been able to provide an acceptable reason for wishing to stay. One which her husband could be satisfied and happy with. She was often aware of her duty as a wife and quite saw that it might include a duty to delude. It had always been the one she was least able to perform.

She had asked herself why she wanted to stay, and got an evasive answer. She did not dare try to analyse it. All she had come up with was that she was experiencing a strong affinity with someone years younger than herself, a total stranger. That much was odd, but blameless. The difference between their ages did not matter. She tried to believe that it would have worked the other way, and if he had been an old man she would have been drawn just the same.

It was not honesty, but a sort of spite which gave her a well-focused glimpse of an old man's ganglion of veins, green and knotted. She had no need to be reminded thus forcibly of the boy's purity and perfection, the just discernible muscles, the down along his cheek. The truth was – a truth beyond which she dared not go – that she could not wish him to be other than he was now. Not so much young, for surely she did not want a Peter Pan, a permanent child, but ageless. Like his manatee, the sort of mermaid.

'You don't really *mind* my staying, do you?'

Her husband said again, with patience – he had decided to be patient – 'Of course you must do as you like. Naturally I should prefer you to come home with us but your mind seems to be made up. We have discussed it enough. Tomorrow we will leave you to your own devices.'

'Devices?'

They were getting ready for bed. Her husband, being ready, lay down and pulled the sheet to his chin. 'Whatever it is you want to do.'

'I shall go for walks.' That was true, though hopelessly inadequate.

'So be it.' He turned into his pillow.

'That thing in Gunhallow church –'

'What thing?'

'The figure-head.'

'Yes?'

'A mermaid, you said.'

'Did I?'

'Mermaids –' she paused, drew breath as if broaching something of great gravity – 'are supposed never to get old, aren't they?'

'I really don't know.' He pushed himself up on his elbow and looked at her with exasperation. She was enough to try the patience of a saint, which he certainly was not. 'It could equally well be a sea-cow.' At that she put down her hairbrush and stood motionless before the mirror.

[85]

She was not doing, or thinking of doing, anything of practical value and he said sharply, 'Melissa, are you coming to bed?'

She came, leaving him to draw the curtains and put out the light. He did not mind, although he had to get up again to do it. She always left him to make the final adjustments to their room before they went to sleep. He surmised, without the incredulity he would once have felt, that if he did not do it she would sleep the night through with the light on. Perhaps because she was afraid of the dark. He got back into bed and touched her cheek. 'Melissa –'

'The boys don't mind me staying.'

'I suspect they're quite glad to be going home. Matthew seems especially glad. If he could be said to have anything on his mind he could now be said to have got rid of it.'

'He worries.'

'About what?'

'Oh – generally. About everything.'

'That's rubbish at his age.'

'He has a worrying nature.'

'Why do you think that?'

'He sees things happen before they happen.'

'Don't we all?' said her husband to her immense surprise. 'Did you know he has a friend staying here?'

'A friend?'

'Older than he is, but from his school, I gather. I didn't know until this evening.' He sighed, though boisterously. 'I've given up expecting to know anything about my children apart from what I can glean. Or other people are good enough to tell me.'

'Staying here?'

'In Tredinnick, I imagine. Matthew asked if I would give the boy a lift back to London. As there'll be a spare seat I couldn't well refuse.'

'But perhaps – suppose he doesn't want to go!'

She was sitting bolt upright, half recoiled, looking down at him. Though all he could see in the semi-dark was the glitter of her eyes, he felt curiously menaced.

[86]

'Really, Mel, you are extraordinary! Of course the boy wants to go. Matthew brought him to thank me. I gather he's short of funds so it's worked out nicely for him, your not driving back with us.'

NO WORD OF LOVE

'Oh no,' said Prue and laughed and realised, too late, that it was the last thing she wanted to do, and was dangerous. What she was laughing at was the irony, the sheer bloody insensitivity; not Menna's of course, for Menna knew nothing. Keeping her in ignorance had been number one priority. 'It would kill her', he had said and Prue had thought that she had no right to be so killable. No one should be able to make it so easy, so expeditious, to commit murder.

'It's only an hour's drive,' said Menna.

'Come with you?'

'We don't have to stay long. There's no point.' Menna suddenly looked quite ghastly.

'I don't think I could bear it.'

'I know it's not your place to, you're not his wife or anything.' But I was, thought Prue, I was something. Would now be a time to tell her: 'Jim and I, we didn't "make love" as they say, we didn't have to, it was a case of love being there already. We loved often and often. Whenever we could, and wherever.' That gave her a place – secret, of course. If she wanted it. 'You're entitled to put him out of your mind,' said Menna, 'everyone else has, his business colleagues, his jolly old pals, and the people we thought we could call on, did call on. Our friends. They borrowed our car and we used their caravan. What are friends for? we all said. But none of them goes to see him.'

To tell Menna now would be inhuman. She had no prospect of ameliorating the knowledge, of seeking and accepting an excuse from him. She would then have to live the rest of her life knowing that her husband and her friend had been lovers. She would use her imagination. And any fantasy she indulged in could, for all she could know, be the truth.

Menna and Jim could not help each other now. He would be faced with her mute reproach. Would it be mute? God knew what she, or anyone, might do in such a situation, confronted, as it were, with an eternally sitting culprit.

I don't want a place, thought Prue. I want to see him whole and corporeal. Not just what God's mysterious purpose has left. The best of him will certainly have been taken. Where? And what for? Where is it now, in heaven or earth? What doing?

'He's quite happy,' said Menna.

'Happy?'

'I suppose because the part of his brain which knew when he wasn't happy, and why he shouldn't be, doesn't function any more. He can sit back and take everything as it comes.'

'What comes?'

Menna still had her moist girl's skin that sweated tears. 'Prue, I can't stand it on my own!'

'There's his sister – surely she goes to see him?'

'Not with me. Alice hates me, she always has. She blames me.'

'You?'

'She says it was the way he lived that brought it on, what she calls his "unbridled passions". I was supposed to bridle them.' Menna, trying to smile, grimaced terribly.

So Prue went. Not out of pity for Menna or love for Jim – love would certainly have kept her away – but simply through being caught off balance.

Menna talked all the way to the nursing home. Prue was a captive listener and she had been away when it happened, had returned after it was all over, bar the weeping. She had not been told and had not asked for the details, she had taken refuge in a cloud of unknowing.

'I did try to stop him. I tried!'

'I'm not Alice,' said Prue. 'I'm not blaming you.'

'She's a dried-up old maid. You know what she said? She said he'd been mishandled, she said if I'd been right for him none of it would have happened.'

[89]

'Alice's notion of right would be disastrous for him.'

'She said he was biddable. Jim, biddable!' Menna omitted to change down on the hill and the car bucked like a rabbit. 'You know what he's like!'

Prue wondered what Menna knew, or thought she knew – poor Menna who 'soldiered on'. Was it Jim who first used the expression to describe, as it perfectly did, her constant, cheerless presence?

'We were getting ready to go out when it happened. He was sitting on the edge of the bed putting on his socks. We were going to supper with the Penrys and I asked him not to drink so much. He said so much as what? Not so much as to lose sight of himself, I said – he does, when he gets really high. But he said the more he drank the more clearly he could see himself.'

'That might be true.'

'So I said it was a pretty good reason not to drink at all. I was actually trying to think what I'd worn the last time we saw the Penrys so that I wouldn't put it on again. It was no use asking Jim, he would only notice what I had on if I was stark naked. But I asked because he could be relied on to say something – you know what I mean?'

Prue did know. He would say something absurd or irrelevant and the absurdity and irrelevance were what mattered.

'He didn't, not that time. But there was a terrible noise, like bones clicking – it *was* bones, it was his jaw dropping. Oh shall I ever forget it!' Menna drove without pausing through a transverse stream of traffic. 'He was sitting with a sock in his hand and his mouth open and his eyes – they were awful, only the whites showing – turned back to front.'

You will never forget it, thought Prue, neither will I. You've put me into the picture.

'I knew at once what it was, I knew he'd had a stroke, you do know these things, but I thought – God, what things you think! – he's not been stroked, he's been *stricken* –'

'Shouldn't you have waited at that intersection?'

Menna looked wildly round and put her foot down. 'When I touched him – I was scared to, I thought if there's any of the lightning left in him –'

'Lightning?'

'The current, force – whatever it was that had gone through him – I thought I'd get a shock. Isn't that crazy? I was crazy. I didn't know what to do, what I ought to do.'

It was all she thought about – what she had felt. Was feeling. What else was there to go on? It couldn't be known what he was thinking and feeling.

'I touched him and he fell backwards. He lay there on the bed and I thought I must give him the kiss of life. But I couldn't think whether to pump and blow together or alternately.' Menna actually bowed her head over the wheel.

'Let me drive!' cried Prue.

'It's all right.' Menna sat up, peering through the windscreen. 'They said, the ambulance men, that he was all out bar his little finger.'

They drove through a town. Church bells were ringing and Prue wondered if he could hear them. 'Are we nearly there?'

'Another five miles.'

They did two of them in silence, then Prue, dreading but needing to know, asked, 'How much, would you say, is he *in* now?'

Menna shook her head. She looked as if she was going to dissolve into her clothes.

Prue dreaded arriving, yet fretted to be there. 'Why so far? Couldn't you find somewhere nearer?'

'No I couldn't. Jim needs country air and quiet and people who care. They do care in this place, they don't just leave them to rot.' Prue shuddered, but Menna was unloading and who could blame her? 'They have rehabilitation courses.'

'Weaving baskets?'

'Why not? If it's a way back.'

Prue couldn't stop herself. 'To what?'

'To consciousness. Obviously you don't realise – how could you? – how far he is from that.'

The road ran through fields of old stubble, a few crows were picking it over. They stooped and peered and shot out their necks like women at the sales. Prue had an awful thought that there was really nothing to choose between anything.

'Some of them do little light jobs. They pack the cutlery for airliners, roll up the knives, forks and spoons in paper napkins ready for the trays.' Menna hauled on the wheel and swung into a driveway. It had been newly gravelled; they roared over it, Menna shouting to make herself heard, 'Someone has to do these things!' But there were trees, avenues of them, and the gold and copper leaves would soon obliterate the toffee-coloured grit. Prue's father, a landlocked man who loved the sea, had always seen a ship in a tree. 'This is part of the forest,' said Menna, 'Worth or Ashdown or Wych, I never can remember.'

'My father used to say an oak was an argosy and an elm was a schooner.'

'These are beeches,' said Menna sharply. 'The hospital is surrounded with them.' She drove on to the grass verge and switched off the engine. 'We'll have a cigarette. You're not allowed to smoke inside, or even in the garden.'

Prue wound down the window. There was a stiff breeze and the trees were pulling on their timbers. The leaves ran along the boughs with a sound like steam escaping. 'I once saw a man fall out of a tree.' Menna kept flicking the headlamp switch. Prue, wishing she wouldn't, said loudly, 'He was killed.' Click, click went the switch. A squirrel ran and froze, ran and froze up the trunk of a tree. Prue was left with something she had never before aired. It was a dream more than a memory. She had grown out of it. When she thought now of her fears and expectations, she had to smile. Even the tragedy was open to question, no one had ever said that the man was dead. She had thought that he ought to be. She was twelve years old when it happened and life was not yet wholly relied on. There were, she had trusted, other things besides.

'They say he's happy,' said Menna.

The young man wore a red shirt. He was a tree surgeon, her father had said. He came in October to cut back the trees in the municipal park. Every morning as she walked to school Prue saw him straddled on high, thrusting his long-handled bill into the withered branches. The trees were old and blighted, they had been dying for years and could go on for years more. Her father said that elms held on to life. The young man did not. Prue, passing beneath his tree, put her head back and stretched her throat to see him. She watched his red shirt patched on the elm's great fan of sky and thought of voyages, of sailing away with him to hot empty deserts where they would be alone. She was frankly desirous.

Once he stopped what he was doing and looked down at her. He did not speak or wave. He was full of himself her father said, up there, close to the clouds, amputating death. But he had stared at Prue as if he would eat her and she exulted because he was full of lechery. Then he flung up his pruning-hook to a higher branch, overreached and fell. 'It looks more dangerous than it really is,' her father said, but the red shirt, with the young man in it, was tossed out of the tree. People ran to him – keepers, passers-by, children, settled round him like flies. Prue ran home, she did not go to school that day. 'Unlucky boy,' said her father when she told him. He was himself holding on to life without a word to anyone, with the crab's claw tightening inside him. 'I wonder what he would have called these. Galleons, I suppose.'

'Who?'

'My father.'

'Why are you thinking of him?'

'I don't know.' It was not intrusive, the way he had come into the picture and brought the tree surgeon with him. Whatever she was about to feel, she would feel for them too. Whatever she was about to have to think, she would have them in mind.

Menna took out her cigarettes. She shook one into Prue's lap. 'Alice says trees use up all the oxygen and that's bad for Jim. But of course any place I chose would be wrong.'

'Is he – has he changed much? In appearance, I mean?'

Menna, who had been about to light Prue's cigarette, snapped shut the lighter and flicked it on again for her own. Prue looked down to find

[93]

that she was taking the cigarette apart. Her fingers split it and shredded the tobacco in her lap.

'What do you expect? He has massive functional paralysis. Yes, I think you could say he's much changed.' Menna took a deep drag and blew out smoke with a raging sigh. 'Oh don't worry, you won't see a monster. Just a dummy.'

They sat staring at each other. Prue knew that she should be thinking of Menna, what Menna was going through, was entitled and required to go through. She couldn't. Menna's emotions were unthinkable, Prue had neither the time nor capacity to think of them. So it was Menna who said – Prue supposed more to Jim than to her – 'I'm sorry,' and, stony faced, started the car and backed on to the drive.

The next bend, as they reached it, brought sight of the hospital building. It was a pink Edwardian mansion. The bricks had been re-pointed – with a scalpel, thought Prue. The paint was clinically white and the windows had a surgical wink. There was a green baize lawn sprinkled with clean beech leaves. She hated it on sight.

'I had to give him the best, the best attention, the best food, the best air. They don't come any better than this, certainly not in London.' Menna drove round to the back of the house and parked on black tarmac tweedily flecked with white chips. 'Of course I can't get down to see him so often –' There was something unsaid. Prue had time to think and to fear it before Menna countered it, fiercely. 'Not as often as I'd like!' and then Prue felt guilty too.

They left the car and went round to the front entrance. There were three different sorts of boot-scraper on the step. Menna used one, though there was no mud on her shoes. In the entrance hall a young blonde sat at a steel and smoked-glass desk. She glanced at her watch as they went in and raised her brows at Prue.

'This is a friend,' said Menna, 'of me and my husband.'

The blonde flicked a switch on the desk and said, 'Ivanhoe?'

Prue looked round, but there was no one else in sight. The blonde, who appeared to have received an answer, flicked up the switch and flicked on a smile of surpassing sweetness.

'Mr Dawson is in the solarium. I think you'll be pleased.'

As they turned away, Prue whispered, 'Ivanhoe?'

'It's the name of Jim's room.' Prue wanted to run away. She feared for anyone called upon to die in this place. 'How could she know what's going to please me,' said Menna, 'short of a miracle?'

'Miracles don't happen.' Prue stopped her, held her arm. Menna flushed, but something besides strenuous colour darkened her face. 'You'd better believe it,' Prue said sharply to the ineradicable child which also waited in herself.

But when she saw him it was not so much a miracle as a nightmare swept away. He was in a long chair, sprawled as he used to sprawl in her bed, drowsy but unspent, his chin on his chest, looking at her. She thought he was. She thought that he had seen her come in and was calling to her across the room.

It was a big room, woundingly bright, with spiky plants, white wrought-iron tables and garden chairs. Prue saw it afterwards. At first there was just a bubble of light with Jim in it. She worried, afterwards, how she must have looked, she hoped that Menna hadn't been looking at her. She reached his side and knelt by his chair. By then she thought he was looking *for* her, that he was having difficulty in focussing.

'Jim –' She tried to take his hands. It was her first actual experience of the incredible damage done. She dared not lift his fingers because if she did she could only put them down again. They were cold as clay. She had never dreamed that a hand without life in it could be so heavy. His eyes weren't looking at or for her. They weren't looking.

Prue looked up at Menna, Menna shook her head and turned away. A starched white nurse brought two collapsible chairs. 'We're very pleased with ourselves today.'

'Are you?'

The nurse looked reproachful. 'Cardiac damage does not mend like a broken bone, Mrs Dawson.' She snapped the chairs apart and positioned them one either side of Jim's.

Now it was Menna who knelt. She laid her cheek on his, slowly moved her face to and fro, brushing his lips with her own. The nurse went away, crackling like a breakfast cereal.

Prue supposed that for what she had done she was to be well and truly punished. Menna's eyes were closed, she was murmuring to him. It was private – bedroom stuff. She held his head in her hands and moulded her mouth on his in a starved and desperate kiss. Prue's heart turned over, so did her stomach.

Menna looked up. 'He's just the same.' Prue forbore to cry, the same as what? Having to think and allow for what Menna meant, or might mean, was part of the punishment. In fact he was a complete reversal of himself. He had had some notable excesses and his face had given them away. Besides passions which were bad for his blood or his muscles or enlarged his pores, he had had a persistent humour which pleated his jaw, and short sight which furrowed his forehead. His had been a marked and readily identifiable face, it had endeared him to many. Now the marks had gone. 'Stroked' away? thought Prue wildly. His forehead was smooth, his cheeks rounded, his mouth tranquil, his big lips laid together in an official mouth shape. There were no whites to his eyes, the navy-blue irises shone, starrily independent of each other, unfocussed. His chin was the colour of lilac.

It was a gratuitous small miracle. Not for him – he couldn't take advantage of it. Was it, then, meant for Menna to say, 'He's quite happy' and for anyone who could to believe it?

Menna got up, fishing blindly in her bag for her cigarettes. Prue had to stop her from lighting up. 'Oh God, let's get out of here!'

'We've only just come.'

'It's always like this. I can't stay.'

Prue stooped and looked first into one of his eyes, then the other. She could not get through the cornea shining with the refracted light all round them.

'It's not him,' said Menna. 'He's not there.'

Prue touched his cheek. 'Jim?'

'He can't speak. They say anything's possible but I don't believe he ever will again.'

'For God's sake –'

'It's all right, he can't hear, he can't feel.'

Prue said, 'Come over here if you're going to talk like that,' and moved to the other side of the room.

'What other way is there to talk? I've got to face facts. I pretend sometimes. Of course I do. I tell myself that next time I see him he'll be able to lift a finger and the time after that he'll wave to me and then he'll say, 'Where the hell have you been?' And in two or three months he'll be home, sleeping with me. And I don't pretend just sleeping, I pretend everything.'

Prue said, 'There's no harm in hoping.'

'There is for me!'

She hadn't meant to be curious or greatly concerned for Menna, but now she saw, with painful clarity, that there would, there must be, harm. She felt the first degree of it in herself.

'Is it awful of me to mind so much? I mind for him too!'

'No it's not awful.'

'We've had it, haven't we? In every sense of the word.' Menna, trying to laugh, made a sound between a groan and a hiss. ' "Quoth the raven, nevermore . . ." Sex was always very good, you see, with Jim and me. It was bloody marvellous in fact.'

'Yes.'

'He was very active in that direction. Hyper-active. Sometimes I used to wonder if I was enough for him.' Prue heard a cry for help. A peacock's cry sounded like that – 'help, help', over and over again. Were there peacocks here? 'Do you think I was,' begged Menna, 'enough for him?'

Prue thought, who in God's name will help me now? Not Jim, Jim was out of it, guiltless, redeemed. And certainly not God. 'Just what are you asking me?' She was shocked at her calmness, her suavity. She wouldn't trust anyone who spoke like that.

Menna leaned her forehead against the window-pane and steamed it with her breath. 'It doesn't matter, there'll never be anyone else now.'

HIS WONDERS TO PERFORM

'Pocket?' said the sister I had stopped in the hall. 'First door on the right at the top of the stairs.' I thanked her. 'Don't stay long. He's sinking.'

'Sinking?'

She repositioned a clean cloth over the object – I suspected a bedpan – which she held in her arms. 'He comes to the surface now and then.'

Architecturally the Hospice is Victorian Gothic set in a belt of Surrey woodland. The arched windows, stained glass and cruciform drain-pipes give it an ecclesiastical air. But I felt impeccability extending to every rhododendron bush and webby Scotch pine in the front garden. I supposed it emanated from the goodness of the souls inside, the sisters of mercy, and those others who, at their points of departure, were free from sin.

I climbed the stairs, each step taking me deeper into the astringency of carbolic relieved by a whiff of boiled cabbage. I was nervous, wondering what I should find.

Father Tom had always been tiny; as children we thought his surname had to be Pocket because the other Tom's was Thumb. When I grew to be a big girl, with acne, I actually envied Father Tom his daintiness, the delicacy of his hands and feet and his pure white skin. He took the part of an Ugly Sister in our Christmas pantomime once and I heard someone say that he was prettier than the Cinderella.

My mother had warned as I left the house, 'You'll see a difference'. Being very young I had not witnessed enough change to allow for it. And Father Tom, whom I had known all my life, had never varied by a hair's breadth: always the same silvery tonsure, saint's eyes in a depth of bone, and one fray mark on the collar of his cassock which had not broken down or been mended in all my twenty years.

I accepted that now he was entitled to be different. I relied on him, on his unfailing kindness and justice, to make it acceptable to me.

I was in for a shock. Intimations of mortality, the passing of cats, rabbits and distant aunts, had not prepared me for the long, slow, last weeks of Father Tom. I knocked on the door and, getting no answer, pushed it open.

Facing me was a bed, black iron, with a white honeycomb quilt. Above it hung a print of 'The Light of the World', beside it was a chocolate-painted cabinet bearing a bottle of Lucozade. On the other side a bentwood chair. I lingered on the threshold. Father Tom seemed to be asleep and for less than two pins I would have crept away and not returned.

Then he spoke. 'It's you.' He did not appear to have opened his eyes.

I said, 'I'll come back –' and added, shamefully – 'when you're better.'

'Come in.'

Faint though it was, it was a command, and I had never disobeyed his. I moved reluctantly into the room and stood at the foot of the bed. A kind of creeping anguish had started in my stomach.

'Sit down.'

In the bentwood chair, looking at him from close quarters, anguish rushed all over me. Something pitiless had been at Father Tom. If 'Pocket' had always been an appropriate surname for him, there was very little left of him now to go into it. He had shrunk on his bones, his fragile bones could barely sustain his skin. There were places where they did not, his cheeks, which had been pink and rounded, were scooped out as if by some fearful spoon. His dentures had been removed and his lips fell into a hole and scarcely lifted out of it as he drew breath. There was a bluish, twilit tinge to his skin and yellowing bristles where his silver fringe had been. Only his ears looked flourishing, laid out on the pillows.

'Well?' he said.

'I couldn't come before, I've been away on this course –'

He was watching me from under his eyelids. 'You didn't come back on my account, I hope.'

'No – well yes – not altogether –' I floundered on. 'I take my State exam next month, that's how I could get away, they've given us a week off to think about it.'

'Don't think you must do anything for me, child. I want for nothing.'

That did not comfort me. Not to want must surely be the end. I looked round the stark white room. 'It's nice and warm in here.' It wasn't, the window was open, letting in raw air.

'Tell me about your studies.'

I told him, babbling at first, then calmed by his attention and obvious interest. He asked questions, moved his lips to what I recognised as the ruin of his old smile. 'I have great hope of you.'

'I will do well,' I promised. And hastily amended, so as not to sound cocky, 'At least I mean to.'

He managed to nod his head. 'If you have the will to succeed, only God can prevent you.'

'God?' I had not anticipated divine prevention; it was possible, of course, so were earthquakes.

'You had better believe it. It will comfort you.'

I felt there was something somewhere not quite right. Or perhaps it was his saying it, rather than the sentiment.

'Father –' I began, and then he did say something out of keeping.

'I am not your father, nor anyone's.'

'You're my father in God.'

His lips lifted, blown on a stronger breath which I thought was a sigh. I told myself it was all part of the difference my mother had warned me about. How far did the difference go? And where would it leave me? I felt I had the right, the need, to ask if I was soon going to be left for ever.

I couldn't ask outright, but I could sound him. I said, 'I shall always know where to turn for comfort,' and I meant to reassure him in case he was worrying how I would manage when he was gone.

He moved his eyebrows, and then the sign of life was restricted to his eyelids. They trembled with the motion of an insect's wings as it hovers. When suddenly it takes flight, if you have been looking too closely and too intently, there is a moment of shock. I was anticipating this from Father Tom's eyelids.

My mother had said, 'He hasn't got much of a room. Not what you could call cosy. I suppose that has ceased to matter to him, and of course the sisters have as much as they can cope with, but I would have thought –' She had continued to think, looking wistful, but not communicating her thoughts. I did now agree with her. I too thought that the things of this world need not have been so soon and so scrupulously removed. A rug on the floor, a comfortable armchair – even if he couldn't sit in it he could have watched his visitors relax – curtains at the window, flowers, a gay chintzy material on his bed-screen instead of the blank white sheeting enlivened by patches of iron-mould. It was as if they were *hurrying* him.

His eyes were wide open, flown open as suddenly as the insect flies away, and I had missed the moment of shock. 'Child, my good child, will you allow me to talk to you?'

'Of course –'

'When you leave here, forget what I shall say. It will be of no use to you. I don't think it can be of harm.' He appeared to be reconsidering that, because he lay watching my face and frowning. Then he said, in a firm voice, 'I need to say it. How many times have you confessed to me?' My heart jumped, I almost got up and ran. His mouth had fallen into its hole and half his face seemed to be gone with it. I think he was trying to smile. He plucked at the sheet across his chest. 'Here's the enemy, here's the devil. I have been afraid of my body and what it could do to me. I saw the beginning and waited for the next move. It was not vanity, there are unspeakable depths. I thought, it can't happen to me. If it does, I thought, if the worst comes, God will provide. Having provided my body with the means to the greatest harm, He will surely provide the alleviation. And if He does not, I will.' Again there was the hint – stronger this time, strong enough to be a statement – of unreasonable doubt. 'I made up my mind that if I were incurably holed I could not allow people to devote their young – their younger – lives to mopping me up. If I should find myself rotting, day by day, I'd finish the process early one morning, leaving a covering note and one last change of bed-linen.'

'You wouldn't – it would be a mortal sin!'

'Immortal, don't you think? Death would not absolve that one. The time came when it was no longer a hypothesis, nor a temptation. I did not feel so prodigal of my days and nights. Flawed though they were.'

'It will be a merciful release, I don't know why that good man should be called on to suffer,' my mother had said unhappily. 'It doesn't seem right.' To me, still unaware of the preponderance of wrong over right, still expecting justice, it seemed calamitous.

I looked, I must have done, hopelessly dismayed, because he said with his old gentleness, 'It is not your problem and I pray that it never will be. I still pray, I cannot break the habit of a lifetime. Besides, praying is company. For what I receive, the Lord make me thankful.'

Was it my imagination or did I see the old glimmer under his eyelids?

'I'll bring you some flowers next time I come.'

'Bluebells.'

'Bluebells? But there aren't any –'

'The best were always in Fellowes Wood.'

'Do you mean Felloweswood Road, where the College of Liberal Arts is?'

'There was no college in the beginning. In the beginning there were no liberal arts, Adam delved and Eve span.'

'I could bring chrysanthemums.' He muttered something. It sounded like 'Chinese', and was not enthusiastic. 'Or a cineraria in a pot.'

'I'm not for burning.'

He did at that moment look calcified, eyes staring out of the old stone lantern of his skull. They were staring at something somewhere that was intimidating and dazzling him. I thought, is he looking into glory at the blessed saints?

The door of his room flew in and a nun entered, shoulder first, like a policeman forcing an entry.

'Mother of God, are you still here?'

I stood up. 'I was just going –' but she ignored me. She went and stood over his bed. 'Here I've been pledging my soul you'd help me with the teas today.'

He was gazing into her face with an eagerness I found mystifying. She was lanky and raw-boned, seeing those nubbled joints and fiery knuckles I appreciated what 'raw-boned' meant.

'Lies on his back like a millionaire all day, and all night too. You'd think he could find it in him to rise up now and then.'

So it was this woman, a nursing sister judging by the white apron over her habit and white kerchief over her coif, who had dazzled and intimidated him – from outside the door.

'Sixteen teas to prepare, and every one a special case.'

Father Tom's voice came strongly from the pillow. 'We all get the same, egg butties and tapioca pudding.'

'And what else might you fancy, your lordship?'

'A birthday cake with icing and two candles on it.'

She made a dive at him, seized his head and holding it against her inconsiderable bosom furiously pummelled his pillows. 'There are those on this earth to whom tapioca pudding would be the answer to their prayers!' She dumped his head back on the plumped and bridling pillows.

I said, 'I must go now.'

'Child, this is Annunciata – my sister in God.'

She said briskly, 'We make an effort when visitors come. We sit up.'

'Oh please don't make him!'

But she had already grasped him under the armpits and was lifting him. Propped upright, his wisps of hair stood out round his head like the bones of a halo. He said dizzily, 'Why did the good Lord give me such a sister?'

'As part of His plan to chasten the sin of sloth in you.'

'Father Tom's not slothful!' I cried indignantly. 'He never spares himself!'

'I'm talking about eternal vigilance.' Which, apparently, she required even of his pyjamas, for she tweaked the collar up round his

[103]

ears. 'I shall bring a bowl of chicken broth and you must take it. I made a bet on it.'

'Who with?'

'Sister Kate. Ten pee at five to one.'

'You stand to lose fifty pence.'

'Not me. I promised it to the battered mothers' box.'

He sighed. 'I have no appetite.'

'What has appetite to do with it? Think of those poor souls' black eyes and broken ribs.'

'I'll try to take something.'

'I'm not betting for a place. It must be to the very last drop.'

'Suppose I just gave you the fifty pence?'

'That would be a sin.'

'Venial, don't you think?'

'Tom Pocket, you can't be adding even a venial sin to all your others.'

I cried, 'He has no others!'

She turned to me for the first time. She had sandy eyebrows and I guessed that under her coif her hair was sandy too. Her face was at once cold and fiery, as if she'd scrubbed up for something antiseptic. There was an impression of crude carbolic, if I didn't actually smell it with my nose I sensed it some other way. She swept past without a word. From the door she looked back at me in anger. 'He means to go to sleep and wake in Heaven!'

Then she was gone and 'The Light of the World' lifted from the wall with the rage of her exit.

I said, 'I thought nurses were supposed to be gentle and kind.'

'She keeps me alive.'

'And that's about all she does! Surely you don't have to put up with it just because she's a nun?'

'Annunciata.' He spoke it with relish, as if he were tasting the name. 'None other. None better. It's none of your business, child.'

'But if she belongs to an order dedicated to charity and she shows no charity –'

'Charity is a hard word. It does not puff itself up because there's no warm blood in it.'

'She doesn't show any love!'

'At my time of life –' he amended, still with that secret relish – 'of death – love changes out of all recognition. And all degree.'

'I suppose –' I was comfortless, but trying for some comfort – 'it passes all understanding.'

'Not quite all.' And Father Tom, little more than a hollow on his pillow, gave me a secular wink. 'Love is a many-splendoured thing and Sister Annunciata is one of its splendours.'

A COMMUNICATIONS FAILURE

'There is nothing else for her,' said the priest. 'Or for you.'

'For me?'

A moment since she had asked him, and through him God, what she had done to deserve such a burden. He had told her that it was punishment for her sin. Whereupon she cited others who, to her certain knowledge were greater sinners than herself but were not called on to suffer as she was suffering. He had replied that she would do better hereafter for having made some requital on earth. 'And having been a little chastised, they shall be greatly rewarded.' But she was ignorant as a pig and could see no justice.

'If it is God's will you shall lose your burden.'

'What will I gain?'

He was visited by his exaltation which he had not brought with him for fear of seeing it blemished. It raised him on golden pinions. He witnessed this woman's glory, contributing to a greater with which his own was fused. Who could say where one ended and the other began?

'You will gain a ladder to God, a path to the kingdom of Heaven.'

'Will that feed me? Clothe me? Pay my taxes?' She was starting to whine. 'Keep me company in my old age?'

'You will not have to keep her.'

She said, with what he knew to be cunning, 'She is all I have to keep.'

'Then she must be a blessing, not a burden.'

'And what will *you* gain?'

He was ready for that. Had he not asked what, in God's name, he could look for? It could be said that he dreamed, that he was ambitious – but not for himself. 'She is God's chosen material. People will come here to look at her; rich and poor, pilgrims, prelates, princes of the Church will come.'

The woman laughed. 'What's there to look at? She don't dance, she don't speak. She can't break her own bread, if I don't do it for her she swallows it whole.' She squinnied at him and he realised, with amazement and disgust, that she believed she was seeing through him. 'Are you going to make out she's dead and don't rot – like the holy martyrs?'

He twitched the hem of his robe aside from the hens that were pecking about the floor. 'She will be a recluse, renouncing the wickedness and follies of the world, dedicating her life to the glory of God.'

'And is there money in that?'

So often he had the feeling that they were not speaking the same language and prayed that she, and indeed all the people in this parish, should understand his, for to speak theirs would be to put his soul at risk.

'Her example will purify and exalt our spirits and the spirits of all who witness it. This village will be celebrated as the place God's hand has touched. Our church and our community will benefit.'

'She's *my* daughter.'

'If it proved to be – a success –' the word was too secular but he could think of no other – 'I should of course see that you did not want.'

'Man does not live by bread alone. Nor woman neither.' She grinned gleefully, showing the black stumps of her teeth.

He wondered, he couldn't help it, why she had been made in the fashion that she was. For what purpose? The answer came that the purpose was his, she was the work he was called to do.

'You'll lodge her in the church?'

He nodded.

'Well,' she said, 'lodge me there too. It will be better than this.'

He looked at the earth floor, the shutters stuffed with straw, the leaking thatch. 'That is out of the question. There is but one small cell in the crypt and she must be solitary, she must be quite alone.' He went over to the heap of rags in a corner of the room. It was winter, late afternoon, and so dark that he could scarcely see the girl lying there. But he had seen her in the light and knew that she looked, could be made to look, satisfactory. 'I shall bring a brown habit if you will wash her face and comb her hair.'

'Isn't that what I'm always doing? I tend her like an infant and she'll be fourteen years at Candlemas.'

'It is important that you understand what will happen. She will leave this world and never enter it again. That is what it means to be an anchoress.'

'How can she leave the world when she's never been in it?'

'Remember that it is at her own request.'

'Request? They all know she's dumb.'

'God speaks for her. He puts the words in her mouth and I hear them.'

'What words?'

'I will magnify the Lord.'

'You're but a child yourself.'

'I'm twenty-five years old.'

She swept the table-top with her hand. The hens rushed forward in expectation of crumbs. 'And were you but five years older, my lord, you should not have her!'

So it was done, to the glory of God and the salvation of mankind. In both contexts it was no sin to hope that powers temporal would recognise him and his church. He had known that his ministry was to be a special one and this, his first benefice, was the lowly step on which his foot was set. From this he would ascend. The hamlet of Malloran, remote alike from centres of learning and good arable land had, for its very wretchedness, been allotted to him, to try his strength and afterwards to affirm it.

Able to see God's hand, he found no incongruity in sending to a neighbouring convent to beg a homespun garment to fit a maid barely grown. Nor did he doubt the circumspection with which he took tools down into the crypt. He meant to do the bricking himself so that even the labour should be his, and the girl installed before her presence in the church was known.

The mother he could not trust. But he trusted her cupidity. He warned her that there were people who would deny the girl's vocation and he did not need to remind her that interference would mean the loss of the food and fuel he had promised her. What else she hoped to gain he might surmise from the way she rubbed the thumb of her right hand against her forefinger with a shrivelling sound which set his teeth on edge. But he had other matters on which to speculate.

The greatest of these was miracles. And why not? Through such humble instruments were they performed. He had seen Clement of Odiham, a foolish, rustic old man, curing epilepsy and the frenzy. And Sister Ventura, who still drew the pilgrims, painfully climbing on their hands and knees to her mountain shrine, had been deaf and dumb. Had he not distinctly heard the words: 'I will work my wonders in thy sight?' Which he had taken – no, he had been *given* – as a promise of miracles.

He locked himself in the church and went down to the crypt. He put a pallet bed in the cell, a chair, and a wooden crucifix on the wall. There was a stone stoup with a drain hole, and as a habitation it was immeasurably better than the hovel where the girl lived.

He started to prepare the mortar. Unused to manual labour, he was soon sweating. His back ached and splinters from the spade handle pierced his palms. He found great congruity in that. But he had not got the mix right, it trickled off the bricks like gruel. He stood staring at the mess. There was a revulsion in his fingers, he could easily have let fall the spade in sheer disgust. Then he heard the Voice: 'There is a time to every purpose under the heaven.'

By nightfall the work was done, the cell bricked up except for a space to let the girl in. Once she was inside he would finish it and totally immure her, leaving the one small opening at eye level to permit a view into the cell and for the passage of her food and drink.

After dark on the appointed day the woman brought the girl to the church. He turned the key in the outer door and led them down to the crypt.

The girl was wearing the habit he had procured for her, with the hood over her head and her head bowed so that he could not see her face. She moved badly, gripping the ground with her bare feet, one arm outflung, fingers spread to contact, perhaps to rebuff, the solid world. Her mother held the other arm and pushed and pulled her down the steps, hissing as to a beast of burden.

It occurred to him that he did not know the girl's name. He asked what the woman called her.

She laughed. 'If your reverence knew, you would make me do penance for it. But she was baptised Amalia.'

Amalia of Malloran, whom man despised and woman abused: the chosen of the Lord. 'For though they be punished in the sight of men, yet is their hope full of immortality.'

He put his hand on the girl's shoulder. 'We must ask God's blessing.' The moment of committal was the moment of consecration. 'Oh Lord, vouchsafe to this thy servant the peace of thy understanding, the light of thy countenance, the grace of Heaven and the power of thy presence —'

'Amen,' said the woman before he had finished. 'And God grant she keep quiet.'

'What?'

'Why, sir, she's young and sometimes she sings.'

He rose from his knees. 'Sings?'

'Nothing bawdy – where would she learn wickedness? Just a noise in her throat – trying to copy the hens, I shouldn't wonder.'

'Take her in, take her into the cell.'

The woman went through the opening and pulled the girl after her. Then she stood, arms akimbo, looking about. The girl kept her head bowed and in the black shadow of her cowl it was as if she had no face.

'Put her in the chair.'

The woman touched her daughter on the chest. It was but a light touch and evidently was their way of communicating, for the girl went at once and sat in the chair.

He seized his spade. 'Now come out.' As soon as she was through the gap he started to close the wall. Conscious of the woman watching, he worked badly and felt himself threatened with the sin of unbelief. 'Go now,' he said, 'but remember, you are to say nothing until I tell you.'

'What are you doing?'

'I am walling her up. There will be an opening to see and talk to her, and to allow food and water to be passed in.'

'When will she come out?'

'She will not come out.' He turned to face the woman. 'She is without sin and in God's house she need fear no evil. The wickedness of the world will not reach her, she will fulfil the purpose for which she was created.'

'Ah,' said the woman, squinnying, 'and what might that be?'

He said coldly, 'She is a chosen instrument, one of the many by which Satan will at last be destroyed and the Kingdom of Heaven established on earth.'

'It's not natural.'

'Natural?'

'She'll be alone in there with none to comfort her.'

'You say she has never heeded you, so how can you comfort her?' He saw that there was now no cunning in her face, only a homely grief such as any mother might feel for her child. 'God will comfort her, she will be in His house, fed and sheltered. Does she not go hungry, and cold, in yours?'

'*I* go hungry, not her.'

'As a daughter of the Church she will not want.' He added, reluctantly, 'And nor will you.'

She nodded. 'The Church never wants.' Angered though he was, he thought it prudent not to rebuke her.

He picked up the rushlight and led the way back up the stairs. He saw that she did not turn again in the girl's direction, and when he unlocked the door of the church she went without another word. It was what he would have expected, would have wished. But what he felt was a sin against charity.

He returned to the crypt and set the rush candle in a niche. The flame rose up, then stooped and almost died in the draught. He also did not look at the girl. What would he have seen? The feeble light scarcely reached the threshold of the cell.

He worked fiercely, even violently, mindful that the candle could not last much longer. Brick by brick the wall was filled in: he had acquired a little expertise and was able to leave a serviceable opening, one brick deep, three in length, just below his own eye level. He himself was tall and remembered that many who would stand to see into the cell would be shorter in stature.

When all was done he set to washing and sweeping the floor. But he had scarcely begun when the rushlight guttered and extinguished itself.

In the dark his heartbeat was loud, it was quite a knocking – he supposed that was due to his exertions. He could see nothing. Above the steps where in the daytime light penetrated from the clerestory, there was no lessening of the blackness. He had a stifling sense of blackness pouring into and filling every crack and crevice, even the holes – especially those holes – in the bricks he had used to make the wall. He smelt the wet mortar and again his fingers shrank from contact with it.

He tossed away the besom. 'I shall bring you food tomorrow.' His voice was returned at once, was almost stuffed down his throat under pressure of the dark. He listened as best he could for something other than the thud of his heart. A murmur, a rustle, the sound of skin rubbed, even a cry he would have welcomed. What was she doing? Was she aware that the candle had gone out? *Where* was she?

His blood ran cold – for no reason except that he had asked that question. He called sharply, angrily, 'Amalia!' for there was nowhere she could be, except behind the wall.

That night he did not sleep. He lay on his bed thinking of what he should say to the villagers. 'As it was not given to the ant to know the minds of men, so it is not given to us to understand the ways of the Almighty. This girl, whom you all know, afflicted from birth, lacking all things, speech, hearing, understanding, is untouched by sin and thereby is whole and perfect among us. On her, God's grace has descended, to her is given the power of salvation, the casting out of devils, the healing of unclean spirits – and bodies.'

Yes, he would speak to them of miracles. For their unbelief was as precious as their belief, it was as necessary to confound the doubters as to reward the faithful. 'The day will come when the lame will leave their crutches outside her cell and walk away, and the dying will rise up rejoicing because this girl has put forth her hand and blessed them.' No, he would not say so much yet, these were ignorant people, and suspicious. They would ask for proof and if it was not immediately forthcoming they would turn on him. He had seen them turn on each other over a handful of grain. 'The day will come when this place will be known as graced by the divine mercy, the compassion of the Mediator, the bearer of our sins, the Intercessor for our souls. Pilgrims will come, the rich and proud as well as the poor and meek, to seek salvation at our shrine. And we ourselves shall know no evil and no fear, none among us shall go hungry or unclothed.'

Surely they would see the advantages such a reputation could bring to Malloran? They would, surely, be able to see their own good? 'Where there is no vision, the people perish.'

He got up from his bed and went outside. In the east the sky was enriched with gold. The Voice spoke: 'I shall light a candle of understanding in their hearts which shall not be put out.'

And the girl, he might have said – would have said yesterday – was the wick. But today he felt her presence. Just how much he felt it he might judge from the way his feet were already moving towards the church. He was, however, prepared to accept her influence, and his responsibility. For what she possessed was a crude power, restless and unaware of its source, perhaps even of its nature.

He must first contain it – which meant more than just locking the church door on her – and then discipline it according to the divine purpose. All depended on him and how he handled this flawed instrument, this girl. It would be the supreme test and his reward would be the pastor's reward, on a scale undreamed of by the average parish priest.

Then and there he fell on his knees. Strength he need not ask for, it was already in him. And wisdom he had, enough for the girl and himself. But he did not find it unseemly to give thanks for what he was about to achieve.

Running across the grass with his young man's stride he felt that everything was possible. Once, he would have mistrusted his ecstasy and done penance for the fire in his veins. Now he knew that it was his due.

The church was filled with the thin cold light of early morning, he entered it like a swimmer. He seemed to have no contact with the solid stone and wood about him, he was in mid-air, a sensation at once perilous and privileged. He had experienced something of the kind as a small child when his father, playing with him, repeatedly threw him on high and caught him in his hands.

He did not kneel to pray, he stood erect, arms opened wide, offering his strength to the emaciated Christ above the altar. He spoke no words nor did he receive any. There was no need. All that he needed he had, and all that he had he was about to give. At the thought of giving what he knew to be worthy, he was filled with a consuming joy. Was he not returning to God His own, His love of mankind and His great design to pluck every soul, even the blackest and meanest, from the fires of Hell?

He made final obeisance before the altar and turned away. The rays of the winter sun had reached the chancel windows. It diminished but could not utterly dispossess the shadows in the crypt.

From the top of the steps he called 'Amalia!' There was no answer, no sound. He called again, and descending the steps, acclaimed her, 'Blessed Amalia of Malloran!'

When first he saw into the crypt he did not, would not, believe his eyes. They were using the dusk, he thought wildly, they and his treacherous flesh, to fright him. For it was what, in his worst moments, he would have feared to see. The fact that he had had no worst moments, had never lost faith, must surely preserve him now.

He moved closer, going gently down the steps as if to avoid breaking a dream. It was in truth an evil dream, the enormity of which he was required to realise to the full.

Part of the wall had been broken down. Bricks and mortar were scattered over the floor. The mortar was in grains, crumbled and hard. But it must have been dislodged whilst still wet – as soon as he had locked the door and gone, the night before. And the girl had done it. From inside the cell she had enlarged the eye-level opening by knocking out the bricks round it. There was a hole big enough to let her head and shoulders through.

Only her head and shoulders. In the opening she hung face down, with her arms – such long arms – almost to the floor. She looked like a rag puppet discarded by the puppet-master.

He took another step down, softly and stealthily – he was not cunning, he was afraid. In the rubble he found the remains of the crucifix which she had taken from the wall of the cell and used to prise out the mortar. The wood was splintered, the cross-piece wrenched from its nail. He wondered, and was sickened, at the frenzy with which she had fought to get free. He looked, sparing himself nothing, at her hands, big hands for her long arms. The knuckles were smashed but the raw flesh had dried and the black blood sealed under the skin. The bruises would never change colour, the gashes would never heal. He had known that she was dead, and now he knew that she would be buried with her wounds.

He dropped the crucifix and ran up the steps. He ran out of the church and over the fields, grassland and ploughed, through hedges and ditches. His heart was thrusting out of his chest. But the Voice, when it spoke, was not in the least breathless: 'This is my beloved son, in whom I am well pleased.'

ROOM FOR ONE LESS

Ted Arthur and Billy Creamer had been friends all their lives, and before they had any lives. Their mothers were first cousins, and lived in each other's petticoat pockets as old Mrs Arthur, Ted's grandmother, always said. There couldn't have been much to choose between the twinkles in their fathers' eyes: Ted arrived on a Monday at dinner-time and Billy on Wednesday of the same week, just as old Mrs Arthur was settling her daughter for the night. Their families lived next door to each other and the walls were thin, so Ted was probably one of the first to hear Billy's voice, that is, if such new babies hear anything.

They were put into the same perambulator to keep each other company. The pram was parked in the Creamers' back yard because in their yard was a tree. It was an aspen and they lay, feet to heads like a pair of kippers, watching the leaves turn white in the wind. Billy always had a feeling for trees.

Ted lived for the day, he woke each morning as if it was the only morning of his life, and went to sleep at night as if he'd done all that he purposed. Billy thought a lot about the future, assessing his chances and the possibilities of situations he might expect to find himself in.

They started at infants' school and sat side by side in Wee Willie Winkie chairs, competing to see who could make his slate pencil squeak loudest. Ted was heavier than Billy but they both had brown hair cut in a fringe. Billy's knees were pure, Ted's were bony and scraped. He took tumbles because he always went at a run and a jump, not waiting to walk. When the other children chanted 'Brillycreem!' at Billy, Ted stopped it at once. He danced round, his fists going like pistons and only one of the girls dared repeat the word. Ted hit her on the nose. Everyone, even the injured party, was charmed by the colour

and promptitude of the twin streams of blood which ensued. There-
after Ted was regarded as a showman.

As they grew older, each was confirmed in his genetic pattern and
they could be seen to be not so very different. Ted was big boned and
plain, Billy was small boned and just as plain. What could not be seen
was that together they made a satisfactory whole. No one knew or ever
suspected how satisfied they were. There was no sentiment involved,
no David and Jonathan stuff. It was a trading, for what either one lacked
the other supplied. So far as Billy could remember – Ted didn't give it a
thought – it had been preordained. There was never any system other
than put and take. It worked as well and as unobtrusively as their
cast-iron digestions and they took it as much for granted.

Ted was uninterested in anything cerebral. Billy, though not intel-
lectual, was smart and filled in a lot of schoolwork for Ted. Ted
behaved as if school was a noise in the head which would soon be
switched off. Billy was bad at organised games and would have been
rated an unpopular swot but for Ted who as team captain always put
him where he might stop an easy ball and seem useful.

Ted was a congenital joker. He did not take anyone seriously, least of
all Billy. But Billy was Ted's private joke and although he could be seen
enjoying it he never tried to share it.

They left school, Ted started work in a betting shop and Billy took a
job at the municipal baths. Swimming was the one active sport he
excelled in. He could jack-knife from the high board and do a length
under water. Ted preferred to horse about, he wouldn't practice and he
disliked the feel of water on his eyeballs. Billy liked the brightness and
wetness and noise and even the smell of chlorine. He really liked being
at the baths. More important, the attendants had time to spare once the
basic maintenance chores were finished. Often there was nothing to
do except wait for someone to drown. Billy started attending night
school, taking a course in television and radio engineering. He used
his free time at the baths for study. He sat in one of the cabins with
his books and cyclostyles spread out on a laundry basket and found it
pleasant to glance up occasionally at the blue water. He was happy,

life was a satisfactory arrangement, work and pleasure – work and Ted.

They met every evening when Billy had finished at the Tech. They spent the weekends together, Saturday morning to Sunday night. Billy watched Ted playing local football and cricket or they both watched international games, ate pizza in the town, took away Chinese food, and beefburgers from Macdonald's, trawled for girls – and threw back the catch. Women's talk bored them but they enjoyed spreading the net.

Ted bought a motorbike, a Japanese fire-eater, and they rode it to the West Country for a fortnight's holiday. Ted had fixed a side-car to the machine; it slowed them down but enabled them to pack in all their gear, including a rubber dinghy. They were nineteen, rising twenty, and in their crash-bowlers and goggles their own mothers couldn't tell them apart. 'Peas in the pod, peas in the pottage,' said old Mrs Arthur as she watched them blaze away down the street. 'Wait till Miss Right comes along,' said Ted's mother. Billy's mother said, 'Right or Wrong, she'll split them.' 'What are you worrying about,' said Ted's mother, 'we stayed friends, didn't we?' Billy's mother said boys were different.

They never cared about the weather when they were on holiday, there was plenty of everything to do. Billy liked to swim, Ted liked paddling the dinghy and they both liked going on the town.

'We could use another twenty-four hours in the day,' said Ted.

'Or another hundred years,' said Billy.

Ted said he wouldn't fancy being Methuselah.

'I wasn't thinking of getting old,' Billy said, 'only of having the time to ourselves.'

'I shan't stand for that,' said Ted, 'I've seen what happened to my grandma. She lost her hair and her teeth and she rattles like a rattlesnake. I'm not going to get old.'

'What will you do?' said Billy.

Ted said he would think of something.

They didn't talk any more about it. They were on Rosemullion Head and Ted went down to the strip of shingle, set up an empty can on a stick and threw pebbles at it. Billy lay on his back looking at the clouds.

They were like atomic explosions, broad-based and towering into the stratosphere and they caused him to think, as if he had been brought all the way here just to do it. Ted, down on the beach, had already got the thought out of his system and was scoring hit after hit on the tin. Billy doggedly thought it through to its logical conclusion. If Ted didn't intend getting old, he might have ten years or fifteen – twenty at the outside. Some people started to break up at thirty. Billy thought of a man who had been in the sixth grade when he and Ted were in infants' school and already he was paunchy and bald as a coot. Ted would have to watch his performance, he would have to decide when he was starting really to age and how much he could take. Ted was good at brinkmanship. But having decided when to stop it, he would have to decide how. Billy couldn't see him working that one out: he would just swan through, as he did through everything.

Chilled, Billy rolled over and put his face into his arms. What would he himself do? He wasn't bothered about being old, he expected that he would be someone else by then, but he couldn't imagine life without Ted. If Ted wasn't around, neither would he be.

Bloody clouds, he thought, hiding the sun. He sat up and there was the blue sky and the sea tilting like a glass and down on the beach Ted was chatting up a girl. She had long hair and wore a flowing, flowery garment down to her ankles. Billy propped himself on his elbows and watched. The breeze kept getting inside her dress and filling it like a bell. Ted stood attentive and still, as he did when a new bowler was opening the innings. Suddenly the girl spun round and round and her dress was sucked into her thighs. It could be seen then that she was big and well shaped.

That was their first meeting with Faye Winslow. She was on a tour with members of her local antiquarian society. 'We're looking at castles and earthworks.' She pointed across the headland. 'There's our Secretary, Mr Chown, and his wife, climbing over the stile.'

'Pretty antique themselves,' said Ted.

'That's not fair. They're awfully well-informed and I'm learning all the time.'

[119]

That was the second thing they liked about her, the way she wouldn't let a bad word pass without putting in a good one. The first thing was more complex. Ted liked her figure, which was full of promise. Billy liked the way her skin suddenly and at absolutely the right junctures produced her dark brown eyebrows and lashes and finished with a church window shape where her hair-line began. Ted liked the way she moved. He thought, privately, that she knew what she was doing and that her slow, fond movements were aimed at him. Life for Ted had been relatively simple and out of incuriosity more than selfishness he assumed that there was only one set of feelings – his own. And he knew, the moment he saw her, how he felt about Faye.

Billy watched her with wonder, much as he used to wonder at the Christmas tree and gas log fires when he was very small. She was as beautiful as the tree and mysterious as the fire which burned but did not consume the logs.

She didn't giggle like other girls, she was serious-minded and frowned when she looked at Ted, as if she meant to get him quite right. Ted was pleased that she was taking the trouble.

Billy knew that Ted liked her, but not how much. They didn't talk about that sort of thing. She seemed to like them both. At their first encounter she had looked up when Billy came down to the beach and smiled a welcome. Before she even knew who he was, the warmth and sweetness were there, and definitely they were for him. Remembering the way she looked up he thought she could have been waiting for him to come.

Ted, for his part, knew that she was sorry for the interruption when Billy appeared. 'This is my pal, Billy old Creamer,' he said. Very proper and polite she put out her hand and asked Billy how he did. 'Been snoring his head off,' said Ted, 'that's what he's been doing.'

'I wasn't asleep,' said Billy.

'You're a tease,' she said to Ted.

'I look facts in the face.' He stared at her and she blushed and said she had better catch up with the others.

'Do you have to?' said Billy.

'I really should. The coach is waiting to take us to Goonhilly.'

'Why,' said Ted, 'what's there?'

'A radar dish,' said Billy.

She nodded. 'And ancient burial-mounds.'

Ted whooped riotously, then was taken serious and stood staring at her.

'I really should go,' she said again.

'Do you want to?'

She gazed back at Ted and this time she laughed, opened wide her mouth and curled the tip of her tongue. 'Not really.'

'It's settled then, stay with us.'

'I can't. They'll wait for me, the coach won't leave without me.'

Ted said to Billy, 'Go after them and say she's met some friends and will catch up later.'

'No,' Faye said quickly, 'I'll do it, I'll tell them. It should come from me. But how will I get back to Falmouth?'

'We're mobile, we'll take you,' said Ted.

That was how it began. They gave up their plans – or rather Billy gave up his, Ted never made any – and went after Faye. Next day the antiquarian society was due to look at mounds and stones on Trewithen Moor. The evening of the day they met her, Ted and Billy, with one accord and not a word spoken, packed their boat and tent on the side-car and drove to the moor. They camped the night and were waiting, in their zipped suits and helmets, sitting cross-legged on the grass when the coach-party arrived next morning. Faye was surprised and pleased, but the antiquarians looked at them suspiciously and two of the old ladies were patently nervous.

'These are my friends, the ones I was telling you about,' Faye said to a man with a head like an ostrich egg. He asked if they were interested in the Romano-British period. 'Naturally,' said Faye.

After that the boys followed the party and Billy tried to listen to the lectures. He wanted to get to know something about a subject which obviously interested Faye. But Ted fooled around and eventually they were asked to leave.

'Why couldn't you act sensible?' said Billy. 'You've spoiled our chances.'

'My chances are OK,' said Ted, 'I don't know about yours.' They stared at each other: it was probably the first time they had stirred their own hackles. Then Ted clapped Billy across the shoulder. 'Don't worry, cobber, I dated her for tonight.'

The question of whose girl she was did not arise as a question. Ted took it for granted that at the crunch she would be his, and Billy, who had received some speaking looks believed that they spoke only to him.

For the time being, they shared her, or rather the idea of her, for their passions had not been thoroughly alerted. Ted's were strong in other directions. He would have fought to the death for the honour of his chosen League Division team but he had no territorial feelings where women were concerned. Billy, once, had deeply fancied a girl whom Ted had designated a piece of shag. Billy had felt humiliated by his own feelings and he was glad, and even proud, that Ted liked Faye.

Getting to see her proved to be an exercise. Ted enjoyed tailing the coach. She was fully booked on the tour, scheduled every day to be in another place to look at another heap of old stones, and if she didn't go, she missed her lunch and tea which she had already paid for. Ted and Billy offered to stand treat. She thanked them kindly and said she'd sooner be independent. Also, it caused comment if she didn't go with the others.

'They're jealous,' said Billy. Faye said they were her friends and she would wish to keep their good opinion. She slipped away to join the boys whenever she could. It wasn't often enough for Ted.

'Pack it in and come with us.'

'Where to?'

'Anywhere you like. Along the coast, Exmoor, Dartmoor, we can go anywhere. There might be something doing in Penzance.'

'I'm going on the coach to Penzance.'

'Come with us. You won't have to pay.'

'I can't ride in that box.'

'It's not a box, it's a side-car!'

'Why can't you?' said Billy.

'I feel as if I'm sitting in a coffin.'

Ted burst out laughing. Billy, seeing how serious she was, kept his face straight. 'All right, you can ride pillion.'

She shook her head. 'I couldn't.'

'Why not?'

'I couldn't sit astraddle like that.' She blushed. 'It's not decent.'

Ted said 'Jesus.'

She rounded on him. 'Please not to use that word in front of me!'

'It's the Bible – OK?'

'You could sit sideways,' said Billy. In the silence Ted could be heard tapping out a tune on his teeth.

She said, her blush deepening, 'They're going out to an island to look at some inscribed stones. I believe I could get out of that.'

'When?' said Ted.

'How?' said Billy.

'The day after tomorrow, Friday. I'll tell them I can't go on the water because it makes me seasick. I'll ask them to leave me on the beach and when they're gone you can come and join me.'

'Great!' said Ted.

'Does it make you seasick?'

'Silly-Billy.' She slipped her hand under his elbow. Someone called 'Faye – Faye Winslow!' and she said she must go because the others were waiting.

'Tell them to go to hell!' cried Ted.

She put her fingers to her lips and passed them out a kiss. 'Friday.'

After that Ted became thoughtful. He was thinking what he would do when he got her to himself. He judged that the time for getting had come, or would come on Friday. He considered himself a fully paid-up male, with all the necessary expertise. He was surprised to find that he was going over the preliminaries with excitement and a certain degree of uncertainty. There would be no time to waste.

Friday dawned wet and misty. They were camped in a spruce wood and woke to a thudding on the canvas.

'Rain!' said Billy. 'It's all we need! They won't go.' Ted grunted and burrowed deeper into his sleeping-bag. Dismayed, Billy shoved him. 'They'll never go to the island in the rain!' But it wasn't actually raining when he went outside, just big beads of moisture dropping out of the vapour which formed and reformed, stealthily, between the trees.

'Heat haze,' said Ted, reaching for the frying-pan.

By ten o'clock they were on the beach, waiting for the boat party. The mist had lifted to a woolly ceiling which just cleared the sea. They could see the island, shaped like a helping of pudding.

'It's a good hour away,' Ted reckoned, with satisfaction.

'We'd best keep out of sight,' said Billy.

'Stuff them.' But when the motorboat came round into the bay he dropped with Billy behind a rock.

Minutes later, the antiquarians arrived. They straggled down the cliff path, carrying cameras and lunch-boxes. The old ladies put up an umbrella. Faye, in a see-through plastic mackintosh, came last.

The boatmen put out landing planks and somehow, with pulling, pushing and coaxing, the party was got aboard. Chown waited behind to address a few words to Faye. His bald head could be seen earnestly nodding. Faye, with downcast eyes, fingered her cheek.

'He's telling her to keep away from us,' said Billy.

'Why don't we go and thump him?'

'With a billiard cue.' They both laughed.

Chown climbed into the boat. Faye waved from the shore. She looked deserted and forlorn and Billy's heart went out to her. So, apparently, did Ted's. He broke cover and ran down the beach. Billy followed. At the noise of their feet on the shingle Faye swung round. She flapped her hands at them. When they reached her side she hissed as if the people in the boat could overhear, 'You might have waited till they'd gone!'

'Why?'

'I don't want them to know you're here.'

'You mean you don't want them to know you're going with us.'

'It will look as if I stayed behind just to be with you.'

'Didn't you?'

'We hope you did,' said Billy.

She tossed her head. 'Perhaps I did, perhaps I didn't,' and took Billy's arm. They went up the beach to the base of the cliff. The mist was leaking and the moisture seemed to be coming from inside out, gentle and private, like a sweat. They blinked to free their loaded eyelashes. 'Ugh,' said Faye, 'how horrible this is.'

'We could go into Falmouth,' said Billy.

'I can't. I must be here when they come back.'

'We could take a walk and find a place to eat.'

'I'm not hungry.'

'We could go for a swim,' said Billy.

'You go for a swim,' Ted said to him.

Fay pouted. 'I want to lie in the sun and get brown.'

They stood in the lee of the cliff watching the motorboat. It had met choppy water outside the bay and was bouncing about.

'See that intermittent flashing light? That's Chown's bald pate sending out distress signals,' said Ted.

'That's not funny,' said Faye.

'Chown's all right,' said Billy. 'He just feels responsible.'

'Does he fancy you?' Ted said to Faye.

'Of course not. He's old enough to be my father.'

'Couldn't blame him even so,' said Billy.

She smiled and pressed her shoulder against his.

'Why don't you go and swim?' Ted said to him.

'No one's going to swim,' said Faye, 'it's too dirty.'

'Why don't we fetch the tent?'

'Tent?'

'We've got sleeping-bags,' said Ted.

'I don't want to sleep!'

'Who said anything about sleeping?' Ted winked. 'We can make ourselves nice and comfortable.'

Billy started up the beach. When he looked round, Ted had closed in on Faye and was walking his hand up and down the small of her back. Billy called to him to come and help. 'I can't carry everything.'

'Don't bring everything,' said Ted, not looking up. 'One sleeping-bag's all we need.'

Billy knew that it was time to ask himself some questions and get straight answers. He didn't want to do either. He would rather have things keep on the way they always were with Ted and himself, he was even ready for them to keep on the way they were with Ted and himself and Faye. But he could see that that wasn't possible. One way or the other the balance was about to be changed.

When he reached the path he turned and looked down at the beach. Ted and Faye had their heads together. They were talking or they were kissing or just gazing into each other's eyes. It didn't matter, any more than seeing a detail of an operation mattered. What mattered was having the operation. He took out his pocket-knife, went down on his knees and spent some time cutting Faye's name in the turf. To one side of it he cut three more letters: 'Ted'. On the other side he worked longer to cut out 'William Creamer' in full. Then he sat on his haunches and looked at the names.

If he expected them to resolve anything, he was disappointed. He had intended 'William Creamer' to be positive and clinching, instead it stayed alone. Ted and Faye paired up. He took his knife and dug out Ted's name. He could see his mistake then: 'William Creamer' was only fractionally himself, it was the official – birth certificate, school-register, electoral roll – fraction. And Billy, just 'Billy', was too much himself. He was shy, almost superstitious, about putting 'Billy' next to 'Faye'. So he dug 'William Creamer' out and left her alone in the grass.

The tent was cumbersome to carry. He took the groundsheet but couldn't manage the bedrolls. Going across the headland he looked for the boat the antiquarians were in. It was the size of a tea-leaf and had almost reached the island.

Ted and Faye weren't on the beach where he had last seen them. They weren't any place where he could see them. He stood at the top of the path and shouted. There was no answer and no movement except the tide bringing in kelp and spreading it over the beach.

He left the tent on the grass and went down to the cove. Pounding to and fro, calling, peering behind rocks, he realised that he was a non-starter. The gulls had their reasons for screeching and the sea was doing its own thing right out to Australia. Up on the headland his name had been dug back into the grass.

He pitched the tent on the cliff top. It was the umbrella type, one punch and it was up. He spread the groundsheet inside and lay down. So what was he doing here? The answer came that he was waiting. For what? For Ted to be finished with Faye. What sort of ploy was that? It wasn't a ploy, it was an excuse. For what? The answer came, for being here. It was the only reason he had for being in this place, at this moment, on this planet. The truth, and he was going to get it whether he wanted it or not, was that he had been dropped, not even like a player after a bad season, more – no, altogether – like a cigarette stub. Ted had dropped him in one second flat, one of those seconds when he was looking at Faye and stroking her back. And it had, he could be sure, taken second place to the looking and stroking. Ted had Faye – technically he was probably having her right now – and the truth of the matter – Jesus, who wanted it? – was that Faye had nothing to say to Billy. The saying and doing was all for Ted.

He shut his eyes. The sun came through and the tent was as bright as a banana. He had not wanted a yellow tent, it woke him too early. Nothing woke Ted.

They wouldn't be going camping after this. Ted would get a car and take Faye to the country. She did not like the seaside, she said it was too noisy: 'You can't hear yourself think'. Billy had understood that she was referring to that sound of something huge and unreliable going on all the time. 'Think?' Ted had said. Billy recalled how she had linked her arms in each of theirs, joining the three of them together and how she had said, 'You never do, do you?' It was what she liked about Ted. Everyone liked it because they knew where they were. Here and now was all there was with Ted. It could be why he, Billy, was feeling like nothing. He jack-knifed upright. He had never believed in psychologists since he realised they started by putting the blame on being born.

Ted, coming across the headland, made straight for the tent and found him sitting cross-legged in the opening. 'Get up. Move!'

'What for?'

'Faye's stuck, you'll have to help me get her out.'

'Stuck?'

'Like stuck in the mud, stuck in a lift –'

'Lift? What lift?'

'Don't just sit there!' Ted hauled him to his feet. 'Do something! Help me!'

'What's happened? Where is she?'

'She's stuck in a chimney, got her foot caught and can't get up or down.'

'A chimney? You said it was a lift –'

'It's not actually a chimney, it's a sort of blow-hole. We were sitting in this cave, on a nice sandy ledge and neither of us noticed the tide coming in.' Ted blinked frankly, 'We were too busy. And when we did, it was too late to walk out of the cave the way we walked in. She didn't want to get wet, and anyway she can't swim. We saw this opening in the rock and went up it. At least, I did and I was nearly at the top before I realised she wasn't with me. I went back and she was stuck half-way and crying her eyes out.'

'What about the tide?'

'Oh she's well out of reach of that.'

'Show me where she is.'

Ted held him by the shoulder. 'No, wait. It's no use trying to pull her up from the top. Her foot's jammed and you can't get past her to free it. The only way is for me to go back into the cave and get up to her from there. When I've released her foot, you can pull her out.'

'I'll do it, I'll go to the cave.'

'You'll likely have to swim underwater.'

'I'm better at it than you.' Billy pulled his shirt over his head, unzipped his trousers and kicked them off. In his underpants he started down the path to the beach.

Ted shouted, 'The cave opening's over there, where the muck's building up.'

Billy could see swags of brown kelp rolling in and heaping against the base of the cliff. There was muscle in the water. It went in under the rock with a noise like an underground train.

He threw his shoes as far up the beach as he could. Then, as he picked his way among the boulders he got the full force of a wave in his back and was shot head first into the cave mouth. He just missed being unsexed by the peak of a submerged rock.

After that it wasn't so bad. The sea seemed pleased to be inside and moved about making slapping and sucking sounds. Evidently it was going to fill the cave before it turned, but there was still room to swim through to the ledge where Ted and Faye had been. He thought about that after he had climbed out and stood pinching the water out of his nose. He saw the opening in the rock above and reckoned the tide would flush into it. If Faye was up there she could drown like a mouse in a drainpipe.

He called her name. 'Faye?' went pancaking all round the cave. There was no answer from her.

Actually it was more of a rocky staircase than a chimney, narrow but quite easy to climb. There was light from the opening at the top. He could see a wedge of blue sky and grasses leaning in.

'Faye?' he said, 'Faye!'

She was sitting on one of the steps about half-way up. She had her arms round herself and her face in her lap. The way she was huddled reminded him of a tramp he had seen kipping in a shop doorway. 'Faye?' he said, shocked. She did not move. 'It's me – Billy.' He went close. She moved then, pushed her face deeper and tightened her hold on herself. He touched her ungently. 'You've got to get out of here.'

She made some sort of noise and started rocking to and fro. Billy suddenly saw himself in his wet underpants down a hole with a girl who was acting funny. People would find it good for a giggle. He had never felt less like laughing. He felt dismay at everything not being what it seemed – especially Faye, especially when he remembered what she had seemed.

He touched her hair, he had often wanted to, now he simply wanted her to get her head up and pay attention. 'It's all right, your foot's not caught, there's nothing to stop you –'

Then Ted shouted from above, 'That you, cobber? Have you got her?'

'She's OK,' called Billy. 'She's only got to get up and come.'

'Hold on.'

The wedge of sky was blocked out, sand rained down and Faye wailed like a banshee. Ted's feet appeared, then his knees. He crouched on his haunches and reached down to her. 'Honey, come on.'

At least it was real with him there, it was really happening. His presence made the situation credible and perhaps later Billy would be able to laugh. 'She's crying.'

Ted put his hand on the back of her neck. 'Listen, you've got to come with us.'

She stopped wailing long enough to say that she couldn't.

'Why not?'

She kept her head down and hiccupped into her lap.

'She's probably got claustrophobia,' said Billy.

'OK, so we'll have to shift her. I'll pull and you push.'

She didn't lift a finger to help or hinder them. They had to manhandle her and she wailed all the time, except when she screamed in protest. Being a big girl, well proportioned, her best proportions did not match the proportions of the passage. It narrowed in places to something less than the width of Billy's shoulders.

One of those shoulders was set against Faye's provocative rump. Not that Billy was in any state to be provoked. Literally bringing up the rear, he struggled to keep his footing and hers. More than once he feared she would pull them both down into the cave. Ted, in front, had her by the hands and could brace himself. Billy, in his wet socks, tangling with Faye's voluminous skirt, his naked back pressed into the gritty walls

[130]

and most of Faye's weight on his neck, definitely had the worst of it.

It was like trying to get born and being prevented – and what did he know about that? Rising twenty, how should he remember being in the womb? The idea was unpleasant anyway, and Faye's presence made it sneaky. As if it was meant to grab him.

Ted shouted, 'I'm at the top – one more heave and we'll have her out.'

Billy made an effort but it wasn't enough. She lay supine, half in, half out of the shaft, unable or unwilling to help herself.

'Get your hands on her tail and push,' said Ted. 'I'll pull.'

Billy actually saw what he himself was doing. He saw it as plainly as if she had no dress or anything else on. He had this clear mental picture of his two hands grasping each a generous cheek which slowly and seductively blushed between his fingers.

'Push!' shouted Ted. Billy pushed. First her thighs, then her legs and feet vanished above his head. The lozenge of blue sky appeared and Ted's face looking down. 'Are you all right, sport?'

Billy stepped up and out into the sunshine, a step was all it was, yet he was sweating steam. From Faye, lying inert and inelegant on the grass, he turned his eyes away.

'Cringe, that was some haul!' Ted knelt beside her and nudged her. 'Honey, you're OK now.'

'She's passed out. She's unconscious, that's what she is. Why did you take her down there?'

'Why do you think? We wanted to be on our own, and I'll tell you something else. It was mutual.'

Faye blinked up at the sky. She looked as if she was getting a message. When Billy leaned over her she did not change her focus, she blinked through him. 'She can't see me!'

'She can see *me*.' Ted leaned down and kissed her ear.

Faye sat up. The first thing she did was pull her dress down to her ankles. Then she looked at Billy.

'You're hurt.' She pointed to the weals on his legs which were leaking blood and water.

'It's nothing,' he said, bunching his wet pants between his thighs.

'Why didn't you follow me up?' said Ted.

'I couldn't.'

'You could have, it was dead easy.'

'I couldn't move, I never could have moved. I was paralysed. I would have sat and died down there.'

They were silent. It was Ted's turn to blink, squatting on his heels, gazing at Faye. If there was a message Billy hoped he was getting it.

'I'll go and find my clothes.'

When he turned his back Ted and Faye saw that his shoulder blades had been scraped raw. He went away across the headland, his wet pants wrapping and unwrapping his narrow thighs.

Faye rounded on Ted. 'Why did you let him do it?'

'Do what?'

'You think I don't know what happened?'

'Getting you out, you mean? We didn't have any choice. It took two of us and Billy's the swimmer.' Faye had gone pink as a shrimp, her eyes brimmed with tears. Ted pulled her to him, kissed and held her. 'You've no cause to worry about Billyboy. He swims like a fish and dives like a duck.' She swallowed a sob; her bosom being against his chest, Ted actually felt the sob go down. 'Honest to God,' he said tenderly, 'he was never in any danger.'

'Why did you let him touch me like that!'

'Like what?'

'As if I was a bundle of laundry!'

'Well, we couldn't wait to ask you how you wanted to be touched.'

'Him, of all people!'

'Who of all people would you prefer?'

'It was utterly humiliating. I have never been so humiliated in my life.'

'What are you rabbiting about?'

'It was indecent!'

'Indecent? Like indecent assault you mean?' Ted hooted. 'Hey, is that what you think we were doing?'

Her lip trembled. 'It was the way he touched me.'

Ted himself had started to redden. 'One of us had to get behind and push.'

She wailed. 'It was *my* behind.'

BISCUIT

The big girl was working on her face as they turned on to the motorway. She had started at Clapham North Side, drawing a mouth and biting off the outline. Her teeth, stained with purple lipstick, turned pink with her saliva. She took a black pencil and sharpened her hair-line. She did her eyelids mother-of-pearl. The car was shaking to bits but she raised her brows and with a tiny brush set about particularising every hair.

Palmer watched her in the mirror. It was the other girl he wanted to look at, but when he reached up to angle the mirror Alec said 'Leave that, I've got to watch my tail.'

Alec's knucklebones splayed over the wheel, his neck sticking out of his shoulders, were a sure sign that he was not his usual self. The sign was needed and appreciated, for Alec seldom had to make an effort or let it be seen that he was making one.

'You mean we're going to look at a *grave?*'

That was Gwen, the smaller of the girls. She was not so small, it was just that the other one was as big as a house.

'We're going to look *for* a grave.'

'You mean you don't even know where it's at?'

'Biscuit knows. What he doesn't know is if he can find the place.'

Rubbing his breath off the windscreen with his sleeve, Alec caused the car to swerve into the next lane. It was sucked up by a passing tanker and the big girl shut her eyes. Looking at her marbled lids the impression was of strenuous weariness.

'Don't be frightened.' Palmer blushed when Gwen giggled. 'Alec's a good driver.'

'If Biscuit was driving you'd be begging for mercy.'

'Biscuit!'

[134]

He saw that they would have their laughter ready for the rest of the day, as part of the good time they were going to have.

'Taking us to look at a grave!'

The smaller one, Gwen, came momentarily into his range of vision. He could confidently say, describing her, that she was pretty. She had everything going for her: skin, mouth, figure, and fronds of hair pricking her eyeballs so that he ached, with rage and concern, to blow it away. She of course would be Alec's. That was a foregone conclusion, concluded the day she was born, or the day Alec was. Alec was born to the best.

'Whose grave is it?' said the big girl.

'We could have gone to Cardiff with my cousin.'

'And a load of frozen cows.'

'My cousin drives for the Meat Market, it would have been better than this.'

'Don't blame me,' said Alec, 'it's not my idea.'

'It's what's-his-name's!'

'Didn't I introduce you? Girls, meet Huntley Palmer.'

Gwen knelt on the back seat and talked sign language to a motor-cyclist in their wake. The big girl leaned forward and something of hers, her hair or her cheek, touched Palmer's ear. 'I'm Darlene.' She reached her right hand, fingers out, thumb cocked, over his shoulder. Dismayed, he grasped it.

'Pleased to meet you.' He should have said 'Hi', and kept his end up.

'I won't go looking for a grave.' Gwen put out her tongue at the motor-cyclist. 'Morbid's not in my nature.'

'It's in his,' said Alec. 'It turns him on.'

He was prepared for Alec to take up the subject and bounce it around. He knew that Alec would have fun with it. 'My grandfather was always talking about this girl. She turned *him* on. She was a music-hall star in the old days. She's buried at a place called Martinhill. I thought I'd like to go there.'

'Nothing wrong with that,' said Alec. 'Everyone spends non-League Saturdays looking for graves of old music-hall stars.'

'We're joint owners of the car,' said Palmer, 'we share running expenses and petrol and today is my turn to choose where to go.'

'Why choose a grave?'

The question had been bound to be asked. He had not prepared the answer. There were a few reasons he could advance, short of the real one, such as wanting somewhere to go and a reason for going. What he didn't want was another trip to the coast, he was fed up with the sight of fruit machines and ice cream kiosks; when he walked on the pier and saw the sea creeping about under the boards it made him dizzy. This afternoon he had determined that they wouldn't go to some raddled old beauty spot in Surrey or Sussex with fifty million other people. 'It's nice country, Wilts.'

'Nice country to be buried in,' said Alec.

Gwen, losing the motor-cyclist who shot past them in the fast lane, cried, 'Just you turn this car around, Alec Prior, and take us home. We're not going to any old bone-yard.'

'No turning on the freeway,' sang Alec. 'Don't worry, girls, you'll love every minute.'

'This girl, Maudie Rochester her name was, used to come on the stage and sit in a swing and ask the audience what they'd like her to sing – ballads, negro spirituals, hymns, opera, anything. She sang the Flower Song from 'Carmen', it's for the tenor, but she had a free-range voice, she could sing anything.'

'Why didn't he bring his grandfather?' demanded Gwen.

'My grandfather's dead.'

'Everyone he knows is dead.'

'It's raining.' Peering through the steadily beading windscreen Alec took his foot off the accelerator and got a vicious blast from following cars. 'Hell, let's get away from this road.'

'It would be nice across country, it's nice country, we'd see the Army badges on the hills. You can see them for miles, dug out of the chalk.'

'He's got a thing about holes in the ground. He should watch himself,' said Darlene.

After the old man died there had been a gap, the gap of the old man, and when Palmer came up against it he had immediately turned away so as not to give it a thought and certainly not a feeling. People said that he had soon forgotten, he and his grandfather had been such friends. He could have told them that he could not forget until he had remembered, and remembering was what he was putting off.

'Why do you call him "Biscuit"?' said Gwen.

'I was brought up to like things nice.' Darlene put her lipstick into her nose. 'We weren't encouraged to be earthy.'

'I was named after my grandfather, Huntley Hubbard. My mother married Jack Palmer, my name is Huntley Palmer.' He saw, through his anger, that Darlene's red nostrils made her look like a rocking-horse. 'Don't talk about me as if I'm not here!'

'Biscuits should be eaten and not heard,' said Gwen, flicking the lobe of his ear. He moved his head aside, she came after him, her third finger triggering against her thumb. It was quite hurtful.

'My grandfather used to take her flowers to the stage door and she always took one out of the bunch and put it in his buttonhole.' He turned to look Gwen in the eye. He had a presentiment that for her he existed only as a thinker and feeler, one who could be made to feel and left to think, but not as himself. Certainly not as Huntley Palmer.

'Look at it rain,' said Darlene. 'Why don't we go to the pictures?'

'Do you want to look at shadows when you could be seeing the real thing?' said Alec.

'What thing?'

'What's real?'

Still wanting to reassure them, Palmer said, 'It's only a shower. Showers and bright intervals, they said.'

Gwen was no longer flicking his ear. She had put up her knees and was pressing them into the back of his seat. He imagined her saying, 'Oh I'm glad you heard the weather forecast, they're usually right, aren't they?' When today was over, when he was in bed, he would make her talk. People said and did nice things when he was in bed. They turned to him gladly, the men in the paint shop called him to join in a game of cards during tea-break – 'He's lucky at cards and lucky in love'.

Old women, alone at windows, had their days made by seeing him pass, they cried 'God bless you!' The ticket-collector who had caught him using an expired ticket and frog-marched him along a platform full of people, knelt at his feet and begged, 'I don't ask you to forgive me but you're welcome to kick my teeth in.' Girls told him, 'I've never met anyone like you', and drew his hand to where it mattered most. Last thing before he fell asleep, the beautiful Punjabi got up from her cash-register at Tesco's and followed him. Tonight, Gwen would rub her face on his as she was rubbing it now, like a cat urging, on the back seat of the car.

'What are you going to do when you find this grave?' asked Darlene.

'I just want to look at it.'

'And what about us?'

'We've worked out something for you,' said Alec.

'Not in a churchyard!' cried Gwen. 'I never have and never will.'

Palmer imagined her beside him at the gravestone – 'In ever loving memory of Maudie Rochester' – and she was saying, 'I think it's lovely of you, it's what your grandfather would have wanted.'

'Gwennie and me will stay in the car,' said Alec, 'while you two go look at the grave.'

Darlene pulled a face. Her lips rolled back over her pink teeth, her nose puckered like a puppy's and the colours she had put on – red, pearl, black, purple – ballooned all over her face. It was not a face Palmer had admired, but he did not like to see it destroyed on his account.

After days of hot weather the ground steamed. 'Fog,' said Alec, 'is all we need.' One of the wipers fell off. They stopped and Palmer went back to find it. A lorry had gone over it and it was useless. Alec threw it into the ditch. 'First place we come to we'll get a cup of tea.'

The first place was a log cabin. On the pitch of the roof was the menu in white painted letters: Meat Pies, Hamburgers, Fried Fish, Chips, Eggs and Bacon, Country-baked Apple Tart, Ice Cream, Hot and Cold Drinks, Sandwiches, Take Away. There was an avenue of privet-bushes planted in converted motor-wheels painted with Sandtex. The

nifty rain ran red, green and fluorescent over a plastic sign which read
'The Peacock Room'. Alec drove between the privets and the silence
rolled over them the minute he switched off the engine.

'I don't like it,' said Gwen.

'I don't want any tea,' said Darlene.

Alec sounded a blast on the horn. Afterwards the silence came into
the car and right into their eardrums, singing like a cistern.

'There's no one here.'

'Look at it rain.'

Alec flung open the door of the car, they watched him cross the
concrete strip and go into the cabin.

Darlene said, 'It always rains on Sunday.'

'It's not Sunday,' said Palmer.

'Did I say it was?'

The silence furred up the windows of the car. Darlene yawned,
opening her mouth to her uvula and demolishing her face again. After
all that work, it showed how she felt. Palmer always looked for what
really mattered to people so that he could count on it. Alec was
beckoning from the door of the shack. 'He wants us to go in.'

'I don't like the look of it,' said Gwen.

'You don't have to worry –'

'Why not? How do you know what I worry about?'

He had been hoping to know. But he could not count on Darlene's
face, she cancelled it for reasons neither momentous nor shattering.
And if there was nothing to count on with her, how much less was there
with Gwen?

He opened the car door for them. The rain was coming as if it had a
schedule to meet and the girls ran across the yard squealing. Darlene
flapped her hands about her face, Gwen twisted to dodge the rain-
drops.

As soon as they were inside the cabin Alec wanted change for the
fruit machine. He snapped his fingers while Palmer searched in his
pockets, it mattered to Alec to keep going, never to be stopped or
slowed down or put out or lost, even for a word.

They were the only signs of life among plastic-topped tables and bentwood chairs. At one end was a counter with a hot-water urn and showcases stacked with pies and sandwiches and chocolate bars. On a shelf behind the counter rows of cups stood upside down in their saucers and above them was a phalanx of Coca-Cola bottles. There was a wool picture of a lady in a poke bonnet and crinoline, and a glossy photograph of a girl naked to the waist, smiling and kneeling to demonstrate that her gourd-shaped breasts reached to the ground.

'This the best you can do?' said Darlene.

Gwen peered at the photograph. 'It's faked, she's got her elbows bent.'

'It's creepy,' said Darlene.

'It's clean and tidy,' said Palmer. 'I expect this is a slack time, just after three, and everyone pushing on. You do tend to push on when it's raining.'

'Gwen and me are pushing off,' said Darlene.

'Where to?' Alec put one of Palmer's tenpenny pieces in the machine. 'Who's going to drive you?'

'We'll sit in the car and blow the hooter till you come out.'

'I don't think you should,' said Palmer. 'It might be misunderstood. Drivers are funny about hooters.'

Gwen kicked the fruit machine and Alec won fifty pence.

'This is a creepy dump,' Darlene said loudly.

'Good afternoon, ladies and gentlemen.'

He had opened the door behind the counter and was leaning against the jamb, smiling; his smile was what they saw first, he had such big teeth, like piano keys. Then they saw his exploding hair and his unmitigated blackness, his pre-shrunk jeans with satin patches at the knees, the bottoms shredded and the sleeves of his shirt torn off at the shoulders.

'You work here?' said Alec.

'In the vacation.'

'What are you vacating?'

'College.'

Alec whistled.

'This is the Peacock Room, he's the peacock,' said Gwen.

'Crow,' murmured Alec as he shot another coin into the machine. The boy could not have heard, he was looking at Gwen and his smile widened until the ends threatened to meet at the back of his head.

'The boss is Mr Peacock, I'm Irwin, I wait at table when he can't get a girl. Customers prefer girls to serve them.'

'We don't mind,' said Palmer.

'Could be an ape,' Alec said cheerfully, 'so long as we get service.'

The boy went on smiling, relaxed and easy, but the fingers of his hand crept up and picked at the slack of his shirt.

'Where are you from?' said Darlene.

'Salisbury.'

'Before that.'

'I was no place before that, except in my egg.'

Gwen laughed and the boy's big lips tightened as if he too was laughing at the back of his smile.

'What are you going to do when you leave college?'

'Write.'

'Write what?'

'Novels and stories. I'm going to be a writer.'

'Oh ah,' said Alec. Darlene raised her eyebrows. Gwen giggled.

'Like James Baldwin,' said the boy.

'He was Prime Minister.'

Alec hit the fruit machine. 'This thing is rigged.'

'Rigged?'

'There's no lemon on the middle roller. It's illegal, you could lose your licence not having three lemons.'

'It's not rigged.'

'It so happens I'm an expert on industrial law. I'll have to report you. Where's the boss, let me talk to him.'

'Mr Peacock went to the dentist.'

Alec sighed. 'It looks bad for you, sonny.'

'I only work here.'

'You're aiding and abetting. Ever heard of an accessory to the fact? The fact is the machine is rigged and you let me put my money in, knowing I'd lose it.'

'Oh give it a rest.' Darlene sat down at one of the tables, picked a matchstick out of the ashtray and started on her quicks.

The boy straightened and looked at each of them in turn. When it was his turn Palmer felt the small hairs stir at the back of his neck. Wanting to give it a rest, he could only think to enquire were they the first customers of the day.

'Meaning what?' The boy, unsmiling now, was polite.

'Only that it's so clean and tidy. You wouldn't think anyone – I mean – when it's so wet outside –'

'He means it's clean and tidy,' said Alec.

'I had a coach party this morning. I cooked ten cans of beans and fifty pieces of toast.'

'I wouldn't mind beans on toast.'

'We'll have four teas,' said Alec.

Gwen went close to the boy and followed the big vein on his forearm with her finger. 'Shall I help you make the tea, Irwin?'

'I'll manage, thanks.'

Gwen turned her finger over and looked at it. Alec laughed. The boy's face broke open, his smile swallowed them. Then he went behind the counter and flipped up the lever of the hot-water urn, separating himself from them by the hissing and blanket of steam.

'Nice kid,' said Darlene.

Palmer asked Alec, 'Why did you shoot that line about being a lawyer?'

'For a laugh.'

'I think he believed it.'

Gwen said earnestly, widening her eyes, 'I don't really like coloureds. I can't help it. It's nothing to do with them being black, I don't like yellow people either. I don't even like white men when they go red in the sun.'

'That's not racism, that's sex,' said Alec.

BISCUIT

They watched the rain. Palmer willed it to stop. The drops ran down the glass, wolfing each other. He knew that the afternoon would be a wash-out. Where had the idea come from in the first place? He had never actually thought I should like to go and see where she's buried. The old man would not have encouraged it, he kept a photograph in his wallet of her sitting on her swing, dressed in skin-tight short trousers and tasselled boots, her arms and shoulders bare, her flesh puffing up between the laces of her bodice. She wore a hat with ostrich feathers: Granddad said the feathers swept the floor when she swung, head down, legs up, gathering momentum. The finale was for her to swing out over the front stalls. It was her thighs, his grandfather said, nobody had thighs like her. Fifty years after they had still caused his lips to shine.

Palmer respected that. As soon as the old man died, Palmer went to his room and took the photograph. When he was asked was there anything of his grandfather's he would like to have to keep, he said, 'He never had anything I wanted', because he had taken the photograph to send after the old man, wherever he was. He tore it up and threw the pieces down a drain. It was what the old man would have wanted, he would not have wanted anyone else to have it. But Palmer got a name among his relatives for being a cold fish.

Irwin brought their teas, carrying them from the counter with his black thumbs buttoned over the saucers.

'What's this?' said Alec.

'Tea. You asked for it.'

'It's dish-water.'

'It's good tea, the same as the monkeys drink on television.'

The girls laughed. Alec asked Irwin if he was looking for a poke on the nose.

'Leave him be,' said Darlene. 'He's doing his best.'

Irwin put the teas on the table, sat back on his heels and looked up into Darlene's pink nostrils. 'You want toast and beans?'

'I wouldn't mind.'

'No. We're going,' said Alec.

[143]

'I fancy a snack,' said Darlene.

'Not here.'

'Know what I fancy? Mushy peas.'

'Only take a minute,' said Irwin.

'Make it two portions, one for my friend. But it must be brown bread.'

'Don't bother,' said Alec.

'The lady wants mushy peas on rye.'

'I said don't bother.'

Gwen said, 'I'll have egg and chips.'

Alec shrugged. 'They're fooling around, they play this game whenever we stop. They order food and when it comes they get up and walk out. Gives them some kind of kick. I don't like to be associated with it.'

Gwen threw her tea at him. He ducked and most of it went down Irwin's chest. His shirt darkened, but on his skin the tea showed up white. He kept his piano smile and so far as they could see he wasn't angry or put out, or even serious.

'Are we right for Martinhill?' Palmer tried to make it sound like an intelligent question. What was wanted was not an intelligent question but something to relieve the tension.

Darlene plucked up the slack of Irwin's shirt. 'It'll soon dry.'

'We're going to look for a grave.'

'When I came out,' said Darlene, 'my mother said "All you girls think about is enjoying yourselves." '

'I told my cousin we were going stock-car racing,' said Gwen.

'We're not sorrowing relations,' said Alec, 'we never met the dear departed. All we know is, she's buried at Martinhill.'

'It's not far,' said Irwin, 'five miles as the crow flies.' He did not blink. On the contrary, Palmer saw their four figures mirrored steady and small in his eyeballs. 'Take the lane to the left past the first round-about.'

'Maudie Rochester,' said Alec. 'Do you know her? She was Biscuit's granddad's girl.'

'Biscuit?' said Irwin. 'That somebody?'

'How could he know her? She was before his time.'

'So was Napoleon.'

Irwin said, 'Napoleon that man sat at the seaside and told the waves to turn around?'

'Come on!' Palmer turned his back on them.

'Before I move from here,' said Darlene, 'I want it understood that I am not walking round any churchyards.'

'Missus Rochester?' said Irwin. 'She the lady that burned down the Hall?'

'She did what?'

'Maybe fifty years ago.'

'Hall? You mean she was giving a show?'

'She did that.' Irwin's face fell into seriousness so quickly and completely that they heard his jaws click. 'She gave the show of her life.'

'My grandfather never said anything about it.'

'She was on the roof, roaring crazy, cursing and crying, with the flames all round her and Mister Rochester down below hollering "Bertha!" '

'Her name was Maudie.'

'That was her other name. Mister Rochester called her Bertha, he reckoned she was a bad one. Give him his due, he went up on the roof and tried to bring her down. She fought him tooth and nail, she had plenty of both, and did her best to push him over. When she realised she couldn't, she let out a screech to freeze the blood and jumped.'

'I don't believe you!'

'Mr Biscuit, she broke up like an egg when she hit the ground. That was some house, three storeys high with a fancy battlement and she was a big lady, picked up gravity as she fell. It's like this: the breaking point of a human anatomy is in direct ratio to the weight of the falling body and the height it falls, allowing for a proportionate increase in velocity per pound – of flesh, that is – for each cubic foot of air travelled. The biggest and the farthest falls the hardest is what it comes to.'

'He's lying!'

'They buried her in the parish churchyard, but you won't find a headstone, her folks don't care to be reminded.'

Palmer cried, 'If it was true, do you think my grandfather wouldn't have told me?'

How could they think? They hadn't known the old man, hadn't seen him holding up her picture to the light, reviving the colours and sounds, glorying again in what the two of them had done together. 'You can't imagine what it was like,' he used to say, 'waiting for her to come on, knowing she was there behind the velvet curtain with the gold tassels, the orchestra tuning up, waiting and watching for the first glimpse. We all loved her and she loved us. That's the difference, the theatre was full of warmth, our warmth. Maudie knew how to bring it out. Nobody can do that now, they can only bring out the bad.' Palmer was happy for the old man to be so secure and certain. He sometimes thought that the old man's conviction of good was the best he himself could expect.

'Perhaps he didn't hear about the fire,' said Alec.

'She didn't die like that, she died young.' His grandfather had said, 'The Lord giveth and the Lord taketh away. Remember that, if ever you get any of the best in life.'

'Missus Rochester was thirty, maybe forty years old.'

'Maudie went into a decline.'

'Decline and fall,' said Irwin.

'What hall did she set fire to? How did she do it? What about the audience?'

'I reckon everyone had a good view. That Hall was a fine big place full of valuable furniture. She lit the beds, old four-posters with curtains, and the whole lot went up whoosh.'

'Beds? In a hall?'

Irwin seated himself at one of the tables and propped his smile on his hand. 'Thornfield Hall.'

'Why don't we *go*?' said Palmer.

'Wait a minute, I'm getting interested,' said Alec. 'I want to know why she set fire to the beds and why there were beds there anyway.'

'They had a bed in every bedroom. Man, I reckon they had more beds than they could use without switching.'

'Bedrooms?'

'Man, I reckon they switched.' Irwin's burst of hair trembled delicately and they suspected that he was laughing. 'Missus Rochester was out to get the governess that was chasing after her husband and she set light to the beds thinking to catch them in one or another.'

'Maudie was never married!'

'Indeed she was. She was Missus Rochester. And Mister Edward Rochester was a black sort of man.'

'Black?'

'By disposition. He had black moods. He forgot his marriage vows the minute he set eyes on the governess, though by all accounts she was a plain jane with a sharp tongue. She had her sights on him. I reckon those two were meant for each other.'

'I don't believe a word of it. Maudie didn't have a husband and she never burned anything down.'

'I could show you the house, what's left. Nobody's done anything to it since. You can see the sockets where the joists were and the timbers stuck up where the roof-tiles were, and a tree growing up through the middle.'

Darlene said to Gwen, 'We could hitch a lift to Salisbury.'

'You should go and look if you're interested because any day now the bulldozers will go in.'

'You're making it up!' Palmer was startled to find how near he came to hitting Irwin.

'Why would he do that?' said Alec. 'It's not exactly a giggle.'

'Can't you see he's made up every word?'

'You know something?' said Irwin. 'I wish I had.'

'My grandfather went to every theatre, every town she played in. He was with her right up to the time she died. She caught a chill waiting on Rugeley Station but she went on for her act. The audience wouldn't let her go. She gave them song after song until she fainted away and they carried her off the stage. She got pneumonia and in a week she was dead.' The old man had liked best to hear her sing 'I Know Where I'm Going'. She made them all think they were the one going with her. 'She wouldn't kill anybody!'

'She had her reasons.'

'She wouldn't kill herself!'

Irwin said soberly, 'I reckon she had a moment's real passion for space.'

'Are you saying my grandfather was a liar?'

'I don't recollect mentioning your grandfather.' Irwin turned to Gwen. 'Did I mention old Mr Biscuit?'

'It would have been in the papers!'

Irwin nodded. 'You'll find a complete account in the public library. The governess, Mister Rochester's lady-love, she lived to tell the tale. Naturally it's biased on her side, but reading between the lines you can guess what the other poor lady had to put up with.'

Palmer felt his pores leaking. He was weeping under his clothes. He turned his back but knew that they would all have seen how his eyes were brimming.

'We'll check you out, son,' Alec said to Irwin. 'We'll go and look for that house. What was the name?'

'Thornfield Hall. You take the first lane to the left after the roundabout and the right fork at the crossroads before the village. The gates are a mile further on, set back in a thorn hedge. There's a drive up to the house. Over the lintel of the door you'll see the words, *"Errare est humanum"* – "Everyone balls things up sometime". I reckon that was Mister Rochester's excuse.'

'What happened to him?'

'He was blinded in the fire but he married the governess and they raised a family.'

Palmer dared not look round. He was weeping all over, his tears were probably showing through the back of his jacket. The only way to hide it was to go out into the rain and get soaked.

'So we're going to look for a grave and a grotty old house,' said Darlene. 'You boys certainly know how to give girls a good time.'

'It's the principle of the thing,' said Alec. 'If we don't find that place exactly as he said, we'll come back and take him apart.'

'I'd come and show you,' said Irwin, 'but I can't leave the café unattended.'

Palmer was asking what the old man would have made of it. He was asking point-blank and without ceremony, for an answer from wherever the old man was. Granddad, your lovely, your one and only Maudie Rochester, your singing, swinging darling wasn't loving or joyful or balanced. She was cracked and vicious, an arsonist and a killer. She didn't die rather than disappoint the audience, she took her own life because she was married to a man who didn't want her. Your memory was groundless, the picture you kept was of a non-person. Better if it had been a picture of a basket of kittens, cats are real. Was that all you knew, Granddad? Was that all you had to show for sixty-odd years – twenty of them mine?

He edged to the door and opened it. The rain had eased off, it wasn't going to help him. As he went towards the car he felt his wet skin stiffen and remembered his mother saying, 'If you put on an ugly face and the wind turns, you won't be able to get it off'. He might surprise them one day: if he ever managed to sort this out he might throw off the crazy things that other people imposed on him, in due time he might cease to be the bonehead who believed everything he was told. For the present time, for now, there was ruination and the consciousness of how badly he had been betrayed. The old man too. But there could be no forgiveness, the old man had been old enough to know better.

'What's the hurry?' shouted Alec from behind. Palmer scrambled into the back seat of the car. Alec, peering in through the window, caught him rubbing his wet cheeks on his sleeve. 'It's OK – we'll go.'

Gwen got into the car beside Palmer and took his hand. 'We'll do whatever you want.'

Tears blurred his vision, he goggled at her like a fish, his right eye let go a drop which rolled as bold as brass down the side of his nose.

'I swear to God if he's kidding us we'll come back and sort him out,' said Alec.

'I'm not bothered,' said Palmer.

'I can't figure him out but I think Irwin's a nice boy,' said Darlene.

Alec switched on the engine and blipped the throttle. 'Why don't you call a spade a spade?'

Impossible for Palmer to tell them what was bothering him. They must be thinking that he was neurotic. He saw how it must look, but to assure them that this was a one-time event which had come like a pain in the gut he would have to own to having a pain in the gut. How could he explain to them what it was about if he could not explain it to himself?

'It'll be all right,' said Gwen.

If only she had said that an hour ago Palmer could have believed her and would have put all of himself into his hand which she was holding in her lap.

'When I get upset,' said Darlene, 'I take deep breaths and think of Prince Charles.'

'Mind you, it'll be a waste of gas,' said Alec.

'You said we'd go and look – you promised Biscuit!' cried Gwen.

'We won't find anything.'

'Of course we won't.' Gwen took Palmer's arm, pushed her shoulder under his and laced their fingers. He had her sympathy and could perhaps have more, but he felt nothing.

'Here's where we turn off,' said Alec.

'Don't bother,' said Palmer.

'First left after the roundabout and right at the crossroads for Thornfield Hall, if you believe that bush boy.'

'I don't care.'

'You've got no principles.' Alec swung the car, tyres yelping, into the narrow lane.

Alec would know, they all would. He was transparent and they looked through him and saw his principles tipped over like a stack of matches. It was a matter of pride really, of not having any of his own. He borrowed other people's. Sometimes it was because of Alec that he held up his head, sometimes it was someone in the paint shop or the

assembly-team or administration – there was plenty of pride in administration. He helped himself from people on television and films, from
DJs and strangers in the street. He had helped himself from that
private source in his grandfather, whose brand of pride had supplied no
one else. The old man had been so sure. It was the virtue of his years, he
said, to know what he knew and to know that all the worldwide rest
could neither profit nor comfort him. Palmer, at his time of life, had
been envious. He had helped himself to the certitude and pinned his
hopes on it. For although what had been good for the old man might not
be good for his grandson, if the goodness, the sureness, had been, it
could be again in another shape and style.

'I'm not a racialist,' said Alec. 'It would be the same if he was a pure
blooded albino trying to get a giggle out of my friend's personal
feelings.'

'They don't have the same feelings as us,' said Gwen.

The old man had gone without a word to anyone. His heart stopped
while he was shaving. He must have had just time to put down his razor
and see what a dying man looked like in the mirror. He left an old body
which they laid out in a starched shirt and double-breasted pin-stripe
with a kiss curl on the forehead. It had as much connection with him as
an empty paper bag with whatever had been in it. Alive, he had been a
rough diamond, scabrous in his personal habits, hot-headed – a lot
hotter-headed than his grandson. Which was why his swift going
seemed right and exemplary, it meant that his gospel was secure.

Alec halted the car and backed it, engine whining. He spun the wheel
to face an opening in the hedge. They saw a muddy track winding away
under trees. There were gateposts but no gate, a ditch brimming with
thistles, and blackberry brambles unrolling like bedsprings. A tree had
fallen across the track and lodged itself in the branches of a tree on the
other side. It looked comfortable.

Alec got out of the car, leaving the door open. The odour of damp
and rotting vegetation made Palmer sneeze.

'Turn it up, old mate,' said Alec. He had no more time for Palmer, he
was not one for mateyness, he liked to be ahead, in the lead. 'Forget it,

old mate,' he would say, and move off towards the better thing he had to do.

'There's the thorn hedge.' Darlene pointed. 'Like Irwin said.'

'Come on.'

'I'm not coming,' said Gwen. 'It's muddy.'

'Well I can't get the car past that tree.' Alec kicked the nettles which sprang back and wet the knees of his trousers. He gestured to Palmer, 'You coming?'

'No.'

'Don't you want to see where Maudie lived?' said Darlene.

'I'm not bothered.'

'You better be,' said Alec. 'You started this, you're going to see it through.'

'It's through as far as I'm concerned.'

'We're all concerned, old mate.'

'You-all can see it through.'

Alec's complexion, which was gingerish, turned meaty. 'You bring us out to the back end of nowhere, waste a Saturday afternoon and a tank of petrol and you're telling us to go and do your business for you?'

'I've got no business.'

'Your business is to find out if there's a burned-out house at the end of this track. Because if there is, your granddad was Joe Soap, and if there isn't, we are.'

'It doesn't matter.'

'Where's your self-respect?' Alec took out a cheroot and spat the end into the bushes. 'I intend to satisfy myself, one way or the other.'

They watched him march along the track, hands in pockets, the cheroot gusting smoke. When he reached the fallen tree he walked up it and dropped out of sight among the branches. They heard rustling.

'He's made up his mind Irwin was fooling,' said Darlene. 'Think I'll go see what there is to see.'

She fastened up her hair in a piece of pink tulle before she stepped out of the car. They watched her teetering over the mud to the fallen tree. She hitched her skirt to her thighs and straddled it. The pink tulle, tied in a bow, was like a pair of pricked ears.

Gwen sighed. 'Why did you do it?'

'Do what?'

'Make up that story about your grandfather. Pretending to be so upset. I'm surprised at Alec swallowing it.'

'Alec?'

'He's not so bright, you know.'

Palmer didn't know, but people often took for granted that he did. 'You know', they said, stating something new or totally unsuspected, and 'yes', he said, snatching at the new notion without even trying it for size. But this time his instinct was to reject the new notion.

'Not as bright as what?'

'As you and me.'

He wondered what degree of brightness was the norm, let alone the ideal, with her. If she was ribbing him she would certainly share it later with Alec. They would laugh, a last laugh, then finito. Forget it, old mate.

'If he really believed you came to look for the grave of your granddad's girlfriend, he'd believe anything.'

Thought, with Alec, was not a private occupation. He conducted it aloud, exposing the processes and arriving in full view at the conclusions. When Palmer had first broached the idea he had said, 'For crying out loud'. He was testing the compression of the car at the time and his surprise could have been at what he was finding. 'It's what I want to do,' Palmer had said. It was something he felt he owed the old man even if, in spite of his advantaged position of being alive and kicking, he was unclear about the debt. 'He didn't believe Irwin.'

'He wouldn't, would he? On principle.'

Gwen started to flick the lobe of Palmer's ear. He moved his head but she followed, diligently firing her finger off her thumb. It became increasingly hurtful and he put up his hand to protect himself. She leaned against him, her eyes at first agonisingly wide, then half shut under her bang of hair. Her tongue, pointed and pink, signalled to him.

Palmer was struck with amazement. She looked like something in an aquarium. He had seen creatures upside down behind the glass, shooting out their tongues. But they had to do it to live. With a sly movement, as if to keep it secret from him, she drew his hand to her breast. He felt nothing, but could think everything. He had severed all connection with his body, had no idea where his arms and legs began, let alone how to move them. He was a thinking head on a non-contributory neck.

'Quick,' she said, 'before they come back.'

Palmer did what he had thought of doing when first he saw a girl with her hair in her eyes: he blew it away, as he used to blow away dandelion-clocks when he was little.

WOUNDS INCURRED
IN THE MATING SEASON
========

Shane asked when his father was coming home. He asked on Tuesday and Wednesday, Thursday he didn't ask because he was away swimming. On Friday he said, 'Will he be back tomorrow?' His father was a long-distance truck driver and Shane wanted his bike fixed. It was an ordinary question but he got an out of the ordinary answer.

'No.'

'Sunday then?'

'No.'

'Monday?'

'He's not coming back.'

'Not never?'

'Not ever.'

Shane's mother picked up the baby and laid her cheek on its bald head. She looked sleepy; Shane had known her eyelids flutter shut, her mouth open, and her and the baby drop off together as if they operated on the same system.

'Why isn't he?'

'How should I know!' She spoke in a complaining sort of voice, but whose fault was it if she didn't know?

'What about my bike?' She moaned, and his heart dived. 'The chain keeps on coming off.'

'Chain?'

'What goes round the pedals.'

'Which goes.'

'Round the pedals. And the sprocket.' He was proud of the word. 'Where's he going to live, then?'

'Lillyhill.'

'He doesn't like Lillyhill. Can't stomach it.'

'Stop talking like that!'

'Like what?'

'Like him – stomach it – oh God.' Her face seemed to melt over the baby's head and Shane thought confusedly that she was blubbing and angrily that she ought not to be. Grown people didn't, not even women.

In the garden his sister Merle was swinging her friend Nelly Greencole. They stopped talking as he approached, Nelly Greencole stared at him from between the ropes of the swing as if he had no business being alive.

He went behind the shed and messed about with his bike. The chain needed shortening and he didn't know how to do it. It would never get done now. He tried, gingerly, to confront the other implications and found that he couldn't, he might as well say the world was ending, and look out for himself. His father drove all over the country, stayed away days at a time, and came back. He always would come back. Shane picked up the bicycle chain and threw it at the wall. 'Bullshit!' Saying that was a huge relief.

When Nelly Greencole went, Merle sat in the swing idly tipping to and fro. Shane moved towards her, also without deliberation, via the gooseberries where he stopped and picked and ate two, although they withered his tongue. 'When's Dad coming home?'

'He isn't.' Merle was admiring her feet. She stretched her legs and contrived to make a dimple appear in her ankle.

'Don't talk dafter than you have to.'

'Run away and play, child.'

Merle was rising twelve, had risen above herself in Shane's estimation. Time was when he would have pushed her out of the swing. A delicacy in her, not in him, prevented him from laying hands on her. 'Don't think you know anything I don't.'

'If you know, why ask?'

'I don't believe it!'

'Oh you,' said Merle absently, giving him a quarter of her attention, or more likely one-eighth, leaving seven-eighths for her feet.

'Where's he gone?'

'He's got a fancy woman at the Cove. If you know what a fancy woman is.'

'I forget more'n you'll ever know.'

'Then you're a dirty-minded little boy.'

Shane opened his mouth and shut it again. A dirty mind depended on what you called dirt; what Merle called dirt other people called natural. And he could ignore the little boy bit because it didn't signify, she would call him a little squirt and a great brute in the same breath if it suited her.

'My Dad don't like women, neither do I.'

Now it was Merle's turn to ignore. She put her ankles away and spoke briskly. 'Her name's Mrs Turner and she lives in a bungalow. Her husband left *her*. They all do.'

'Do what?'

'Men,' said Merle, showing her eye-teeth, 'are all the same, wanting a change. Dad takes over Mrs Turner and Mr Ricks or Fred Tickner or Billy Gee will take Mam. Whoever doesn't take Mam will take Mrs Tickner or Mrs Gee or Mrs Ricks. That leaves one to go.' Merle sniffed with laughter. 'Mr Turner might come back and *he* might take Mam.'

'I won't have Ricks or smelly old Tickner or Billy Gee or bloody Turner. I'll kick them out!'

Merle began examining her arms which were bloomed with golden hairs. 'It's called wife-swapping, everyone does it but it's only just catching on here.'

'Not here! I don't want it here!'

'You can't stop progress.'

'It's not progress, it's adultery!' He was pleased with his vocabulary until he realised that adultery meant being adult, and therefore he would in due course have to do what his father and the other men were doing now.

Merle found something inside her elbows, she was always searching herself. 'Nelly Greencole's cousin goes to Lillyhill Unity where the Turner kids go.'

'Kids?'

'Nelly's cousin told Nelly and Nelly told me.' Merle shrugged. 'I knew all about it before Mam did.'

Shane's face flamed. 'What kids?'

'The girl's my age, the boy's name is Jerry.'

'What sort of name's that!'

'It's better than Shane.'

'It's Pisspot, a jerry's a pisspot.'

'Don't be vulgar.'

'I bet he's not as old as me!'

'Everyone's older than you.' She turned her arms to see if what was in her elbows went through to the other side.

Shane found his weapon. 'You're like a monkey in the zoo, always picking at yourself!' and he cut away through the garden before she could get out of the swing.

'They're'nt better than us, are they?'

'Who?'

'Mrs Turner's kids, the ones he's left us for.' Shane sat opposite his mother eating egg custard and banana, a treat provided for his tea which at the time of eating compensated for a good deal.

'I'm sure they're not.'

'Why's he gone then? I can't understand it.'

'Neither can I.' Shane wasn't surprised at her helplessness. His father was as strong as a lion and didn't like anyone else to be. 'Is it me,' she said, 'is it something I've done?'

He didn't think so. She was always glad to see his father come home and never offered him a cross word, even when he put his dirty boots in the sink. 'I expect he wanted a change.'

'Yes, but why? No one wants to change if they're satisfied and if he wasn't satisfied was it my fault? Didn't I –' She looked at Shane as if she were falling, and not knowing how to catch her, or even if he should try, he bent over his plate. 'I asked him why that woman's husband had left her – not that I thought it would do me any good to know, but I felt I had to know everything. I would have gone on asking him why all night, only he wouldn't stay, he wanted to get back to her.'

'Them kids,' Shane nodded with enormous scepticism, 'must be really something!'

'I said was it another woman and he said no, Mr Turner just went and lived with his married sister.'

'He couldn't stomach that Jerry.'

'That made it worse, there being no one else.' She leaned across the table and stopped his hand as it was taking a spoonful of egg custard to his mouth. 'It was worse for me, you see.' She didn't seem as if she could see, but wanted Shane to. He did his best when she talked to him like this, she had no one else, his father being away so often and Merle and the baby were no use. 'You see,' she said again, 'if that man went, for no reason, with no – temptation – just because he was fed up, it doesn't say much for Mrs Turner, does it? Yet she's preferred, which says still less for me. Do you see what I mean? I haven't a leg to stand on.'

Her face was melting again, losing its shape, yet somehow still looking like her, so terribly like that Shane was alarmed. 'You're all right, so are we! Me and Merle are better than those kids he's gone to.'

'I asked was it because he was sorry for her and he roared at me. He said he was sorry for a lot of people but he wouldn't change his life for them. But he's breaking up our lives for her and I ought to have told him. I didn't think of it at the time and now it's too late. He's never coming back.'

She held Shane's hand, stopping him from finishing his pudding. She had forgotten about his pudding. When she forgot, and he had to wait for her to remember, he became impatient and recalled her any way he could. This time he had a share of what she was thinking and tried to keep up with it. 'Who says he's not!'

' "I'm not coming back", he said, and took his flannel shirts for the winter.' She gazed at Shane, blinking and breaking tears which somehow managed to join up again and rolled down her cheeks in entire drops. 'What did I do wrong?'

[159]

Shane thought they must all have done wrong because his father hadn't, his father could do anything and anything he did was right.

The baby in its carry-cot broke wind from both ends at once, a commanding performance, rounded off with a dribble which ran over its chin, not in drops like its mother's tears, but in a milky mess.

Shane said disgustedly, 'I can understand him wanting to leave *that*.'

'Half return to Lillyhill.'

'You mean you're under age?' The conductor, pretending amazement, winked at the other passengers.

'I'm rising eight.'

'Does your mammy know you're out?'

'I'm an orphan.'

'That's bad luck,' said the conductor, the grin slid off his face and he gave Shane his ticket.

Shane sat back with confidence. He had told no out-and-out lies: he was seven years and two months old, which was rising to eight; he had lost his father and that was orphanage. Everybody had a mother, you couldn't be born without one.

He had gone about the business sensibly, first enquiring the fare on the bus to Lillyhill, then taking a fifty-pence piece out of his mother's purse after she had given him his pocket-money and so wouldn't be likely to look and miss it right away. Him not being at school that day she would hear about, and when she did, he would tell her – he would have something to tell by then – why he had taken the money, and she would see that he had done it for them all. They had to know, even Merle had to know, why his father had left them.

He was making himself comfortable, wedging his knees into the back of the seat in front when he realised that a fat woman was talking about him.

'Orphan or not, he shouldn't be going about on his own. No one's safe nowadays, not even little kiddies. He could be taken away and interfered with. It doesn't bear thinking about.'

'Come and sit with us, duck,' said a woman in dark glasses. 'We'll look after you.'

'I expect I can find a toffee in my pocket,' said a very old woman, and began turning back her skirts.

Shane felt like spitting with rage. They might make him go with them, they were bigger than he was and there were three of them.

'You can sit on my lap,' said the fat woman. 'I'm going to Lillyhill.'

The old woman held up a wrapped sweet. 'I wouldn't wonder if it's liquorice.'

'You're not shy, are you?' When the other woman took off her dark glasses she had green rings round her eyes. 'Tell us your name.'

Shane said, 'I'm going upstairs. I want to smoke.'

They made a noise like a crowd of chickens and Shane ran up and sat at the front of the bus where he could see everything. Presently the woman with the green rings came to see if he really was smoking. Shane stared at her. She went back down the stairs and he had peace for the rest of the way.

He had been to Lillyhill before, riding in the cab of his father's truck. A footy little place, his father called it. Some of the houses had straw roofs and windows criss-crossed like the jam tarts his mother made. A stream came through the main street, running over Pepsi tins. On the other side of the hill in the new town the bungalows were built round a shopping precinct with a superstore where you could buy jeans, cheese-and-onion crisps, and Go-Cat, and push it round in a trolley-basket. Shane, who meant to get things straight, had to admit that there was nothing to compare with it where he came from.

He walked through the precinct, past the kiosk which sold ice-cream in eight flavours and six colours. He gave it one glance.

A man with a T-shaped gadget was cleaning shop windows. Shane stopped to watch, pleased with the neat way the gadget first soaped the glass then razed it clean.

'Well,' said the man, 'seen enough?'

'Where's Unity Road School?'

'Follow your nose, first right. Late, aren't you?'

[161]

'I wouldn't go to that school if you paid me.'

In a bungalow garden he saw a gnome fishing in a bucket. He considered it a backward sign. There could be nothing to fear from people who had got no farther than such baby stuff; the gnome might even be in Mrs Turner's garden. His lip curled with untempered scorn.

Lillyhill Unity was bigger and newer than his own school building. It was of liver-coloured brick, to twin with the shopping precinct. There was a television mast, cycle sheds and a football field. Shane noted the advantages. Although they weren't likely to be of direct advantage to his father, they added up, he had to look at all of it. Shane looked and was obliged to kick the school railing to relieve his feelings with other feelings. He was wearing sneakers and every kick jarred his leg.

A bell rang inside the building and some boys came into the yard. They were bigger than Shane but he continued kicking the railing. If the pain in his leg couldn't stop him, they certainly wouldn't. One of them strolled over and said, 'Pack that in.'

'Who says?' Shane pulled himself up on the railing until he was eye to eye with the boy on the other side.

'I do.'

'Your name Jerry Turner?'

'What?'

'You look like a jerry turner.' The boy made a snatch, but Shane dropped off the railing out of his reach. The other boys started bouncing a ball and with a vigorous gesture of the fingers at Shane the boy ran off to join them. They all went round the side of the building to the playing-field.

Shane did not have long to wait before the rest of the school streamed out for mid-morning break. The yard filled with boys and girls, the air with their shouts and shrieks. They fought, they battered up and down, clawed and chased each other, danced, some climbed on the roof of the cycle-sheds and drummed with their heels. Three boys turned another one upside down and shook him.

Shane watched, finding in himself a satisfying detachment. He had been part of that sort of thing in the past, but was pleased to think that he had grown up and out of it, and shouldn't wonder if it showed. He beckoned, with a casual jerk of his chin, to a girl who was looking his way. She came to the railing, put her forehead on the bars and stared. Shane asked where Jerry Turner was.

She blinked, confirming what Shane had heard, that the female brain grew a centimetre a year until the age of fifteen when it was exactly half the size of the male and stopped growing at all.

'He goes to this school so you know who I mean.' She went on staring and Shane said sharply, 'You deaf or something?'

'What's your name?'

'Show me Jerry Turner and I'll tell you.'

'That's him.' She pointed.

'Where?'

'In the Barry Manilow shirt.'

Shane put his face as far as he could through the railing. He saw a boy bigger than himself, fat, wearing the short pants and long woollen socks that Shane had put off in favour of jeans and tank tops. Jerry Turner's hair was the colour of straw and he wore wire glasses. Shane was ready to bet that he had wire round his teeth as well.

He watched Jerry Turner go into a corner of the school yard, slowly slide his back down the wall, sit with his knees up and put his thumb in his mouth.

'What's your name?' said the girl.

'Barry Manilow.'

Shane found an empty tin and kicked it to the bus stop. When shoppers in the precinct objected he lowered his head and butted through them. He was in a rage, dismayed and perplexed and needing to take it out on the world.

What the hell – he said aloud 'Hell!' to a woman who squawked when his tin hit her ankle – was he going to tell his mother? He couldn't answer her question, nothing had been explained. So where had they gone wrong? Perhaps the Turner girl was better than Merle, that wouldn't be so difficult. And his mother didn't always say the right thing. Not that they had rows, sometimes Shane felt that his father would have liked a row; sometimes when he came home, full of fun, Shane's mother seemed scared of him. 'Mike, please,' she kept saying, 'please, Mike,' with no more idea than the man in the moon what he pleased. It made Shane's father angry, which was understandable. Mrs Turner might be more fun.

On the bus going home he narrowed the question. Although Jerry Turner didn't look much – about point nought nought one per cent of nothing – in some unseen unseeable way he must be better than Shane. It didn't stand to reason otherwise. Where had Shane gone wrong? He loved his father and when he came home it was the top of the world, it was the way of life and Shane wanted no other. But it struck him with stinging force that what was enough for him might not be enough for his father. Climbing the apple tree wasn't enough for Merle. She used to be good at it and climbed higher than Shane and got the biggest apples. Now she wouldn't even pick them off the ground, she said they were dirty. That was because she was growing up, his mother said. His father being grown up, it must stand to that same reason that he wouldn't want or enjoy the things Shane wanted and enjoyed.

It was an unthinkable thought, but it had come to stay. Dismayed at the thought that thinking could get out of hand he slid to the floor of the bus and crawled under the seats. A man rolled up his newspaper and hit Shane on the head with it. Shane opened his mouth to say something, but the man had a snake tattooed on his arm. Its tongue flickered on the big vein that ran down from the man's elbow.

Shane found that he was going to blub, had actually started. He had hoped and believed that he was over that sort of thing, but the old system still worked, his nose pricked as if it was full of fizzy lemonade, a lump came into his throat and tears were making snail marks all over his face.

The bus drew up outside his school. He looked into the classroom at his own empty desk. He couldn't see himself going back there, he couldn't see himself going anywhere, because anywhere he had been he had been someone else, someone who was good enough to have a father who came home.

The man with the snake on his arm said, 'Dry up, kid, you'll get more than a tap on the nose before you're through.'

Shane gave him a steady stare, snail-shine and all.

When he got off the bus his digital watch registered half eleven on 12th September 1983. The watch had been a Christmas present. He wasn't likely to get any more because between last Christmas and last week his father had gone right off him, off Merle, off his mother, and the house where they lived. Shane couldn't see any future there. But perhaps he wouldn't have a future, just days going on and on like they always had. Only they wouldn't be the same days.

He stayed in the park until school came out, then he ran home. He was hungry and it was dinner-time.

The first person he saw was Merle. She put her finger to her lips. 'You can't go in.'

'Why not?'

'Shhh!' She was whispering, although they were at the front gate and a DC-10 was thundering over, very low. 'They're talking. I hope.'

'Who?'

'He didn't know what to say, he just stood and looked. So did she.'

'Dad? Dad's come back?'

Merle shrugged. 'He's probably just come to pick up his long johns.'

'Let me in!'

'No. You're not to go in there. They've got to talk.'

Shane tried to push open the gate. Merle held it shut. 'You want him back? Then leave them alone. She's got to say something. If she doesn't, he'll go back to Mrs Turner.'

Shane dived through a gap in the hedge. Merle moved fast, but he dodged her and ran round to the back door.

His father and mother were standing either side of the kitchen table. His father was leaning his hands on the table, and Shane's mother was shelling peas.

'Dad?' They took no notice. Shane pulled at his father's trouser-leg. 'Are you coming back?'

'Am I?'

He seemed to be asking Shane's mother, in the wheedling voice he used to the baby. He picked up her hand and curled it round his finger as if it was the baby's hand.

Shane couldn't make them out. He thought that Merle could be right, and if his mother didn't say something his father would go away to Mrs Turner. He shouted at her across the table, 'He's coming back!'

She gave him the merest glance as she lifted her head, her eyes passed his way, passed over him and on up to his father's face. 'I don't know why you went,' she said, 'and I don't know why you've come back.'

'Isn't it enough that I'm back?'

'How do I know you won't do it again?'

'You don't. But this is now and this could be as long as we'll live. Why worry about next time?'

'I can't help it.' She wasn't saying the right thing and she was falling again, falling and beyond help.

'Look, I've got a tanker outside, I'm going to Plymouth and I've left it along the road. You don't leave four thousand gallons of oil un-attended. What I'm saying is, I could lose my job!'

'You'd better go, then.' Blindly, she reached for a pea-pod. It was empty, her fingers searched in vain for the peas. 'I'm getting the dinner.'

The last thing Shane would miss was his father's anger. It would come out of the blue, or out of some bit of black that Shane saw and she didn't, and having come, it would rip through the house, rip them all off and leave his father torn and terrible and alone. His father was angry now, he drove his fists at the table and shouted, 'Is that all you're going to say!'

'You don't want to lose your job.'

'Aren't you pleased I'm coming back? By God, I think you're sorry!'

'It's just that I couldn't bear it to happen again and I'll always be afraid it might.'

'I'm not sorry!' cried Shane.

[166]

His father made a big effort, drew a deep breath. 'I'm coming back because this is where I belong.'

Shane thought that went without saying. He wasn't surprised when his mother looked to him for help. He said, 'I'm one hundred per cent bucked.'

His father turned round and hung over him. 'You are? Why?' Shane had the feeling that they were both waiting for him to help.

'Because it means the other kids aren't no good.'

'Any good,' murmured his mother.

'Kids? What kids?' said his father.

'The Turner kids. They're not as good as us.' Shane could not contain his triumph, it blazed forth, eclipsing them all. 'They're not half as good as us and that's why you're coming back.'

'Am I?' said his father. 'Is that what bucks you? Because it makes you better than them?'

'Mike —' said Shane's mother fearfully.

Shane's father laughed, he looked more like a fox than a lion. 'It's as good a reason as any.'

THE DAY'S RAGE,
THE NIGHT'S REGRET

Major Machin proposed with fairly relative emotions: alarm, dismay, reluctance. No joy. His wife, Luise, was keeping on at him to remarry. When he said, 'Will this one do?', she did not reply. In death as in life, having persuaded him to a course of action, she left it to him to implement.

He had been savouring his widowerhood, gently trying the world for size. It was less than a year since Luise had died, he had still to identify what he was missing, let alone how far he cared to venture. The first he knew of remarriage was a thought slipped into his mind like an unwanted circular, and surely not a product of his mental processes. He took it as evidence of Luise's continuing concern for him and for the concern he was grateful. Although it came from the other side of the grave he, on this side, employed logic, and it had been logical to suppose that she did not wish him to remarry.

By whatever agency – he was unable to say even imprecisely what it was – she proceeded to disabuse him of that supposition. Intimations came with increasing frequency, sometimes as commands, sometimes no more than a nudge, which he might have given himself. If he had, it was due to her infinitely skilful (and she was now infinite) manipulation of his thoughts. When he was driven to cry, 'Will this one do?' he meant for her purpose, he knew what it was, and appreciated the general principle. The details alarmed him.

Something he had missed and was now enjoying was solitude. Without being gregarious or even sociable, Luise had wished for company: her own, she said, was bad for her. If his active services were not immediately required and there was not another magazine he could fetch, window to shut or open, pillow left unplumped, wavelength to be adjusted, his presence was. Luise kept a bell by her side: she had taken pains about the tone. 'If you are to be summoned by bells, my darling, it shall be pleasantly.' When she slept, and when he did, the sound of the bell, rarefied, almost celestial, echoed through his dreams. Luise, it could be said, was with him when he was not with her.

Since there wasn't time for them both, the Major had had to forget himself, in a purely altruistic way, so that solitude, when it came, was an agreeable experience. He was in the process of reacquainting himself with his own capacities, indulging his preferences and relishing the small sense of sin it gave him. Then Luise made it known that she wanted him to marry.

The one who might do for whatever it was that she had in mind was a small, mostly plain girl with chapped cheeks. Major Machin had encountered her in the local supermarket when his wire basket became enmeshed with her trolley and they had to work to disentangle it. The next time, they found themselves waiting at the same check-out. She gazed at him and shyly murmured. On the third occasion he would not have noticed her were it not for a long-standing resentment he had against people who took trolleys when their purchases would have gone into a basket. He felt the same about people who drove around solo in cars, polluting the atmosphere and causing congestion on the road when in nine cases out of ten they could have used public transport or, better still, their feet. Each time he saw this girl she had but two items in her trolley. 'What a nice day,' she said. It was in fact not nice, it was 6 November, cold and drizzling, with the smoke of last night's bonfires still burdening the air. He smiled out of politeness. To his surprise she blushed. He saw that her cheeks were not chapped so much as streaked red, like the little Worcesters he used to scrump when he was a boy. 'Excuse me, I have forgotten my calf's liver,' he said, and walked away. He had been savouring the prospect of liver and onions for supper. He was a good cook, had been obliged to master the art after Luise had her stroke, and was now able to minister to his own tastes.

Contemplating the frozen offal he realised that the items in the girl's trolley had been the same each time: a tin of soup and a wrapped loaf. Young people had better things to do than cook. And remembering her youth he was prepared to give her the benefit of it when next they met. Which was not for several weeks, and by then the Major, having briefly remembered, had readily forgotten her.

But there she was in the street, wearing a cloak which the wind was whirling unkindly. Suddenly the garment was whipped over her head and she was struggling in a kind of tent. The Major watched, amused, then his better nature, never far removed, came to the surface and he went to help her.

'Oh,' she said, gazing at him and seeming appalled when he had lifted the thing off her head, 'I didn't think –'

What didn't she think? She began slapping down the cloak as if it was a boisterous animal. The Major raised his hat, 'The wind is very strong,' and turned away.

There it might have ended, were it not for a coincidence which was really no more remarkable than their other encounters but the more remarked because it was exclusive. One evening there came a ring at the Major's doorbell. On the step was the girl. He said in surprise, 'You!' It was hardly polite, but he was experiencing the slight impatience which sight of her occasioned. She had a tray of paper flags slung round her neck and a collecting can in her hand.

His surprise was unequal to hers. She turned pale, swallowed, and audibly gasped. With an almost panic-stricken movement she shook her can at him. 'I'm collecting for the Royal Lifeboat Fund.'

It seemed to the Major supremely absurd that a small ineffectual female should be raising penny pieces against the might and fury of the sea and he could only repeat, 'Lifeboat?'

'I have credentials.' Now she was crimson with shame, setting down the can, she pulled a printed card from her pocket.

He said, 'I don't doubt, of course.' Their acquaintance was too slight for him to invite her to question with him the congruity of human endeavour. 'I have some change upstairs, will you come and wait inside while I fetch it?'

She would, she stepped over his threshold wide-eyed and spell-bound. What did she expect – Aladdin's cave? Bluebeard's? When he came down with the coins she was standing in the hall looking rather like a castaway herself. 'It's a good cause,' he said, dropping a fifty-pence piece into her collecting-tin. 'One never knows when one will need a lifeboat.'

'Do you often go on the water?'

'Not if I can help it.'

'I love the sea.' She said a curious thing, 'I'd sooner die that way than any other.'

After she had gone, he found that she had forgotten to give him his flag.

When next he saw her in the supermarket it was that last remark of hers and the way she passed by the meat, eggs, butter and vegetables that prompted him to bid her good morning, though he might have escaped unobserved because she had her back to him, choosing a tin of baked beans as if all the 57 varieties were there on the shelf.

'Oh –' He wondered why he always came as a surprise, if not a shock – judging by the colour which rushed into and receded from her face. Her breathing was visibly disturbed, even to his vision, which was fairly perfunctory.

'I have bought some chicken thighs,' he said sternly, 'and am proposing to make a curry. Will you join me for the meal?'

At the time he had no motive, ulterior or otherwise, for asking her. He meant it kindly, insofar as he meant anything; he had not reached the degree of exasperation to which Luise eventually drove him. He didn't even want the girl's company, he was simply reverting to the habit of putting himself second. That was almost certainly Luise's doing.

'Curry?' the girl said faintly.

'Of course if you don't like it.'

'Oh no – I mean yes I do – yes –'

'If you have a previous engagement,' the Major clapped his heels together, parade-ground fashion, 'perhaps another time.'

'I haven't.'

'But you don't care to accept invitations from strange men.'

'Strange?' she cried softly, and it was the Major's turn to feel a warmth, unwonted, beneath his skin.

'Very well. About half seven. I think you know where I live.'

He quite enjoyed the evening, his enjoyment being tempered by disappointment at the way the rice turned out. He observed, as he brought it to the table, 'Indian rice should be dry, each grain separate.' The girl asked if he had been to India. 'One doesn't have to have been in order to make a decent curry.' Although his annoyance was with himself, she seemed to accept the rebuke. 'I don't know your name,' he said sharply.

'Abby Kennard.'

'I'm Edward Machin. How do you do?' He nodded across the table. 'A little late for introductions, but better now than never.' Was it? She didn't recommend herself, the way she was hanging her head and biting her lip. He wondered just why he had asked her to come. 'Is Abby short for Abigail?'

'No, for Gertrude.' A conversation-stopper if ever there was one. He ate some of the rice and made a grimace of distaste. 'I don't like it,' she said.

'I don't blame you. It's a poor effort and in cooking there should always be achievement. No one wants to eat a try.'

'I meant my name – oh dear – it's not – Gertrude's not your wife's name or anything is it?'

It struck him that she was in a vacuum as regards his circumstances and she had a right to a few facts. 'My wife is dead. I was invalided out of the Army in '76 with the rank of major.'

'Invalided?' She gazed at him, fork stilled, a lump of glutinous rice stuck to the prongs.

'A spot of lung trouble,' he said briskly. 'Soon cleared up.'

'Oh.' Obviously unaware that the rice should have fallen softly, grain by grain, not adhered to itself, she ate everything, including the sweet – tinned apricot and ice cream – with genuine enjoyment. She was not a connoisseur, nor even fussy. Luise had been a perfectionist by nature, and hypersensitive when she became ill.

'Wasn't she beautiful,' said the girl, looking at their wedding photograph on the sideboard. The wistful note in her voice did not arouse his sympathy. True, her own looks were unmemorable, he could not recall her face or figure from one encounter to the next: true again, he hadn't tried, but she had the supreme advantage of youth. Naturally, she didn't appreciate that.

'Luise was a handsome woman.'

'So were you! I mean – you were handsome too.' She cried, as if prodded, 'You still are!'

He made a deprecatory noise and folded his napkin. 'Will you take coffee?'

'What about the washing up?'

'Later.'

'Please let me help.'

'I serve decaffeinated so there will be no risk of your being over-stimulated and unable to sleep tonight.'

'Nothing keeps me awake – it used not to.' She seemed to feel the need for honesty and although she coloured up again, she looked at him with a kind of valour which he could not interpret. He judged her to be in her early twenties, newly broken out of the mutinous teens into a formed, or formulating, self. The Major, who was forty-eight, remembered that period of his life as the time of greatest expectation and the only time he had confidently expected to fulfil it. 'Please,' she said, 'let me help you with the washing up.'

Since it appeared to be important to her, he allowed her to accompany him to the kitchen, and gave her a tea-towel. She stood beside him at the sink, drying the dishes as he washed them. It was a deceptively domestic scene, any uninformed person would take them for father and dutiful daughter. He felt completely incurious about her. It was enough to have her there. But he saw that she felt the lack of questions, she could not tell him about herself without being asked. 'I developed the habit of not sleeping,' he said, 'of relying on catnaps while my wife was ill and needed constant care.' And constant cheerfulness, constant concern, constant love. Constancy. 'She could sleep only in the daytime, she felt safer then.'

NO WORD OF LOVE

'Safer?'

'She was virtually helpless. Paralysed from the waist down.' He felt it his duty to state it in so many words, although Luise never would. She called it her Problem, with the initial letter in the upper case.

'How terrible.' Abby Kennard pressed the tea-towel to her breast.

'We had a system,' he said, swabbing a plate. 'It worked, though it was time-consuming.' The system had consumed everything, the love, the cheer, the care, their own selves. 'Without a system she would have existed only as a vegetable. It was designed to give her the maximum advantage, in her limited circumstances, of every moment of every day.'

'How wonderful –'

'We evolved it by trial and error.' Wearisome trials, nerve-snapping errors. 'We lived by it.' In the end the system had come first, taking precedence even over Luise, who was stretched and sustained on it as on her own skeleton.

'What was the system?'

'Each moment of the twenty-four hours was provided for, taken up if not filled, and with allowances for changes in her condition. It did change. Sometimes she was very weak, sometimes she was very angry.'

'Angry?'

'Nothing was interminable, not even pain. I won't give you the details, they would seem trivial.' He could not have borne that. It would have been a betrayal. 'She used to say, "Time is not on my side".' Saying it, he heard not his voice but hers, still shocked and incredulous. He swilled the water in the sink and pulled out the plug. 'That's done. I'll make the coffee. Or would you prefer tea?'

'Oh no, I only have tea for breakfast.'

It was to be about all he learned about Abby Kennard that evening, for she said, 'You must have loved her very much,' and he found that he regarded it as a challenge rather than a statement of fact. Was he, at this late stage – surely it was too late? – being called on to justify all those mapped-out moments, and the hours spent spending them – on what? On ensuring that they were not missed, that not a second got away unobserved. Yet they were not memorable, the thousands, the millions

– even in her shortened space of time there must have been millions. Who had they been saved for? Not Luise who was dead and could not remember: not for him, the only one who could or would remember. What would it profit him to relive any of them? 'My wife was a woman of great natural delicacy.' It was surprising how anyone with such a gross disability could continue to be so delicate. Of course it had complicated matters. Personal functions which ordinarily went without saying had not only to be said, but organised and witnessed. Filling the moments. The Major, who did indeed remember some of those, said to Abby Kennard, 'It was not always enough.' She looked at him without understanding. How could she understand the enormous care that had gone into finding acceptable euphemisms? 'Take me to the bathroom' when Luise wished to be helped to the lavatory and hoisted, dress unadjusted, on to the seat; 'Time for my toilet' meant soaping flannels, rinsing sponges, anointing sterilised gauze and sprinkling surgical powder on what she called the 'distressed areas'. He was not to be reminded, doggedly refused, of a kindred act – sprinkling pepper on the brussels sprouts. The analogy was neither whimsical nor charming and Luise, poor girl, had found it increasingly difficult to be charmed.

'Let me set the tray,' said Abby, and took down cups from the dresser.

He heard Luise's protest, 'We never use those for coffee'. He switched on the percolator. 'Illness heightened her sensibilities. She could not eat food which looked like food. I served her steamed fish in scallop shells, and saffron rice. Potatoes I whisked with the white of an egg and piped on her plate. Meat nauseated her.'

'A chop? What could you do with a chop? Or sausages?'

'Meat *en masse* was unacceptable. The animal origin had to be concealed. I minced it and flavoured it with herbs. Sprinkled with parsley and set among fresh green vegetables she could sometimes be persuaded to eat a few grains.'

'Was she a vegetarian?'

'She wanted everything to be right.' The Major said wryly, 'In a wrong world it took some arranging.'

[175]

'It took trouble.'

'My wife had her fair share of that, Miss Kennard.'

Her lips and eyelids trembled. He was surprised and a little vexed that she minded so much. 'Won't you make yourself comfortable in the sitting-room?'

She went, looking as if she could never be comfortable again. Next moment he had another surprise, unqualified. Luise's voice said, 'You must marry'. It was a direct instruction, spoken in the same tone as 'You must come at once when I ring', 'You must pad out the hollow in my back', 'You must warm the spoon', 'Only boiled water'. He looked at the cups which Abby Kennard had put on the tray and which were not the ones Luise would have used, they were in fact breakfast cups. He did not change them.

When next they met it was in the park where she was eating sandwiches, brown bread and cheese – probably processed. They had made no assignation. It was a fine day and she had taken her lunch to the Billy Ross seat by the pond. Billy Ross had been a local man, a lover of ducks, and the seat had been put up to his memory and theirs. Major Machin, taking a stroll, gravitated towards it because from there he could see St Paul's. He surprised Abby with her mouth full. She swallowed and hastily pushed something into a paper bag. The Major, having lifted his hat, stood looking at the solid bubble of the dome. 'In a few years' time it will be impossible, even from here.'

'What will be impossible?'

'The trees will have grown tall enough to obscure the view of the City.'

'Oh.' He made as if to raise his hat again and move on, but she touched the bench beside her. 'Won't you sit down?'

'It would be an intrusion on your lunch-break.'

'I'm not – I was feeding the ducks.'

He sat down and they watched the ducks and she threw bits of her sandwich. She told him that she worked in the building just across the park. Her parents were dead, her childhood home was in Beckenham and she now rented a room in the house of a distant cousin. She went to dressmaking class and was learning to make herself a winter coat.

The Major listened politely. He felt obligation but no great interest in her circumstances. Although not a selfish man he was at that moment thinking of himself in relation to Abby Kennard. He wondered what he saw in her, he did see something. There was a light at the end of a tunnel: what she was showing him was the tunnel.

'I've never been abroad. I've never been anywhere.'

He recognised one of her outbursts of honesty and valour and murmured, 'It is not necessary,' to console and encourage her.

'It was the first thing they asked when I went for a job as receptionist in a car showroom. They said, "Have you been to the Continent?" I don't see why.'

The Major, who had simply meant that foreign travel or her lack of it would not influence his opinion, ventured something about foreign cars.

'They didn't ask if I could drive.'

'Can you?'

'I'd have learned. It would have been a nice place to work. I liked the smell.'

'The smell?'

'Like coconut. It was the new cars.' Across the park a clock struck twice. She stood up, again as if prodded. 'Will you come to tea with me?'

'I haven't had my lunch yet.'

'On Sunday?'

She looked scared and defiant. He smiled. 'I thought you only had tea for breakfast.'

'At four o'clock!'

'It's very kind of you, but perhaps –'

'I'm late – I can't stop.' She ran away across the grass.

He called 'Miss Kennard!' but she ran on, stumbling and pitching. Even her back looked scared.

He picked up the paper bag she had dropped. There were a few crumbs in it. He took them to the pond and fed the ducks.

After that, Luise made her wishes known, sometimes directly and categorically, more often by a kind of seepage. She had always been able to do that, even at respectable distances. While he was changing her books at the library he would become aware that she urgently needed something at home. Now, in her privileged position, she not only reached him through airspace, bricks, mortar, furniture, trees and moving vehicles, she imbued them with her wish. So that any object, any emptiness, could urge or plead with him to marry and reproach him because he would not. He was accustomed to feeling guilt because he had failed her in all but small things. The cups of tea he had carried, the hot-water bottles he had filled, the hours reading to her at night and sitting with her by day could not atone for the fact that he was well and she was not. He had also accepted responsibility – who else would? – for the fact that the whole world was well and she was not.

Her reproaches now were gentle, almost shy, but came from so many sources that it was like being followed by a sigh. 'No!' he declared aloud, more than once, 'I'm happy as I am,' and the word was claimed by her voice crying from her wheelchair or her bed, in pain, despair, prisoned in her unlively flesh, 'I want you to be happy!' While asking forgiveness for the thought, he accepted that she had a right to his unhappiness, to reach out from the grave and exact it as retribution. He knew, none better, what his sin against her had been.

It was brought home to him when next he saw Abby. Three weeks went by after her invitation to tea. On the afternoon in question he had watched the clock, thinking she might realise her omission and get in touch. When she did not, he put the incident out of his mind. He had much to answer for, but not that.

Abby appeared beside him one Saturday at the library check-out. He wished her a good day; he was pleased because he had just found a new Le Carré on the shelf.

'You didn't come.'

'No.' Searching for his library card he sounded unconcerned.

'I had tea all ready.'

'Ah,' he found the card in his wallet.

'I waited.'

The librarian raised her eyebrows. She was a ripening blonde and looked first at Abby, then at the Major.

'I waited hours!'

Major Machin, who had waited years for what was best described as a sense of alienation, said, 'I'm sorry, I did not know where to come.'

The librarian smiled. Abby made a choking noise and blushed.

It was the librarian's smile, performed by her ripening lips, which concerned him. This young woman whose sole advantage was that she was coming to fruition – if she had other advantages he didn't know them and they were irrelevant to this moment – had just discounted Abby and himself. As she would an unsuitable remark. And with the smile went his alienation, for Abby's distress, though unsuitable, was real and relevant.

'Let us repair our omissions,' he said, 'Mine for not coming and yours for not telling me where to come. Have tea with me now in the town, or coffee if you prefer.'

'Oh no – I mean it doesn't matter –'

He put his hand under her elbow and with a confidence he would prefer not to be feeling, steered her away.

Prepared to settle without a fight for whatever came his way, he realised that it was Abby Kennard who had come. He put up a small struggle, asked himself could he be said to have encouraged her? Had he gone beyond the ordinary politeness demanded by circumstances which he certainly wasn't responsible for? The answer was undoubtedly yes. Inviting her to supper, talking about Luise, must have led her to think of him as more than a stranger. How much more depended on her temperament, and from what he had seen it was not equable.

His own feelings were mixed. His single blessedness was gone, every day waking without compulsion, noticing his whims and indulging some of them, neither envying nor scorning other people's commitments. On the other hand, he had known it couldn't last and that he might not always want it to. It would have been too much to expect the end to come when he was ready and not a moment sooner.

He looked at Abby and saw that hers was a boneless face, the features smudged and undecided. He noticed it the more because Luise's face had been all bone, and every arch and plane and cavity of the structure known to him. Abby's hands looked boneless too. Her fingers crept about, dislodging the spoon in her saucer, touching her lips and trying, without luck, to coax forth words. Her nails were grubby and seeing him look at them she plunged her hands into her lap.

'It was a natural oversight,' he said, 'as much mine as yours. More mine, in fact, I neglected to ask for your address. I hope you did not make preparations.'

'No, none.' She spoke fiercely and he guessed it was a lie. 'It was my fault.'

Luise had said, 'I blame myself. My darling, you think I don't know how you feel, tied to a woman who's only half alive? Tied to a wheelchair? Married –' lightly mocking, disowning the words – 'to a leaking bladder?' From her, such plain speaking was a last straw. It meant that she had come to the very end. When, understandably, she came to the end of patience, strength, the wish and the obligation to live, he used to sit beside her while she slept. *Au fond*, it seemed he was a violent man, and he touched his depths when she touched hers. The room roared with violence while she slept, blindfolded to keep the daylight out.

Once, she awoke, and as if there had been no interval of sleep, spoke out of her depths. 'I want to be a wife to you,' and held up her arms. 'Oh my darling, shall we try?'

She had a silk scarf across her eyes and couldn't see his face. He got up from his chair and went out of the room. He was cold with shock, and sickened. The coldness passed but the sickness increased with the time he had to think. Luise saw nothing and said nothing, but he knew that she knew what he felt.

'My cousin washed the front steps,' said Abby. 'That shows what a muddle the world's in.'

'Does it?'

'Me not telling you where to come, you not coming, and my cousin washing the steps because she thought you were. They hadn't been washed for years and she finds out they're green marble and now she wants to move house because she says green's unlucky.'

The Major had an idea, it was the only one, that Luise wished him to remarry because she didn't like the way he was living. It would not have been her way. She had loved extremes. She had loved it when he was posted to the Middle East, and when they had to come home, as the train carried them through the Garden of Kent, she cried, 'This cold green country is only fit for cabbages!'

'I trust I shall not be the cause, even indirectly, of disrupting your cousin's life,' he said. 'Or yours.'

'Mine?'

'You live with your cousin.'

'Nearly everything that grows is green,' she said stoutly, 'how could it be unlucky?'

When he asked would this one do, he was thinking of what was due to Luise. She had been a beautiful woman of great sensibility. The beauty and sensibility were gone, but the criterion remained. It was all he had to go by. Abby Kennard's looks certainly did not meet Luise's standard and he doubted if her sensibility did either. Also, she was young enough to be his daughter.

He had virtually no choice. His circle of female acquaintances was hardly a circle: it consisted of two married women – friends of Luise's – her masseuse, an octogenarian aunt, and this girl. And Luise having made her mind known, he knew it in his bones, in the things he touched, faces he saw, and in his sleep. But she gave him no indication of what she thought of Abby.

By the time he proposed, he was himself disrupted, his modest isolation lost, and he couldn't drift for trying. He had no feelings about Abby, not even compunction. She was at liberty to say no, and he hoped that his having asked might a little relieve the pressure on him.

Abby said yes. Several times. While he was still hearing, with incredulity, his own voice saying, 'Will you marry me?', 'Yes,' she said, 'oh yes, yes.' She lifted her face and he saw her ordinary blue eyes widen and darken. He kissed her on her forehead.

They were married in a registry office. He did not want what she called their 'engagement' to go on for long. The intimations continued to come, and the reproaches. Exasperated, he rounded on himself, waking in the night, swearing, 'I am going to marry!' but it was as if he had done nothing. It might mean that Luise did not care for his choice.

He had difficulty relating to Abby's idea of the situation, which was simply that of a girl getting married. He had to accept that there was nothing simple about it, for her it was a time of great complexity. If she was to be believed, it was the most important time of her life. She said it was the most wonderful, and Major Machin tried to see the wonder in it.

She was in love, and she let him know it with that valiant shyness which he might have found endearing were it not so misplaced. They were both unprepared, his state of mind as mixed as hers, in its different way. Whereas she had everything to learn, he knew it all. And he knew that he was caught. The old captivity. Perhaps that was what was required of him. When she said she had never loved anyone before, he thanked her. He couldn't think what else to do, what else he wanted to do. But he could see that she had thought of something.

Should he tell her it would be a platonic marriage? The truth was that he did not know what sort of marriage it would be. He had known one sort and could not imagine any other. He could not imagine marriage at all with Abby Kennard.

He thought of leaving. Several considerations prevented him: where would he go, and how long for? When would he come back? He could not escape from Luise's insistence, he would take it with him, like the plague, and probably be plagued into contracting some other mésalliance. Also he could not persuade himself to jilt Abby. He could imagine her distress. Without conceit, in fact with alarm, he thought that it might ruin her life, of which she had so much more to live than he.

The only guests at the ceremony were Abby's cousin and her

husband, and Luise's masseuse, a woman of great *joie de vivre* who kept winking at the Major and declaring that he was doing the 'right thing', as if he had already compromised Abby. The cousin and her husband regarded him with justified suspicion. The cousin said, without hope, that she hoped they would be happy. The cousin's husband said that Abby was old enough to know what she was doing, but his handshake carried no conviction.

After the ceremony Abby, who had been mostly plain, became wholly pretty. She was radiant, as the Major supposed brides ought to be. Luise, he remembered, veiled in white, had kept her emotions hidden, and when the veil was lifted she appeared serene and un-moved. Only when she was alone with him did she reveal her happi-ness.

Abby did not want to know where they were going for the honey-moon – 'Anywhere will be wonderful.' The Major, feeling autumn in his bones, settled for somewhere warm.

'I know the very place,' said the travel agent. 'In the Red Rocks south of Toulon.' 'Is it quiet? I don't want anywhere rowdy.' Although perhaps he should: rowdiness, fun, life, whatever you called it, was for the young. Abby was young. 'The little place I have in mind is much favoured by our clients of maturer taste,' said the agent. 'I think I can promise you a relaxing and delightful vacation. The beach is secluded, quite private, the bathing excellent and the hotel – more of an auberge – offers every facility, and accommodation of a very high order. At the same time it is ideally situated for excursions to the Littoral and Italy. Or there is another place –' 'This one will do,' said the Major.

They took the night flight and arrived at the little place just after dawn. It would have been bigger were it not wedged between two bulwarks of rock. All around it umbrella pines and agaves leaned at angles to the sea. The corniche road, mercifully, was higher up. The Major wondered if traffic, misjudging a bend, or skidding, ever came plunging down on the hotel roof.

He was cold and tired and felt vulnerable. Abby, from the top of the rustic steps down to the hotel, turned to him crying, 'I've never seen anything so beautiful!' It was one of those times when that plundered coast looked the picture of innocence. The light, or lack of it, made tender ghosts of blocks and pylons; the villas melted to a luminous pearl, the rocks were rose rather than red; the sea, breathing like a child, slipped softly between the islands.

'Aren't you tired?'

'Tired?' She was shocked, and it occurred to him that for her being tired meant being bored, not weary. 'I've never been any place like this before. Oh there's so much I haven't done, you must think I'm a fool!'

'No, I envy you.'

It was true. As he watched her run lightly down the steps to the hotel level he wished that he could keep unimpaired at least his first glimpse of this place. Years ago, Luise had derided the extravagances of the Côte with a barbed wit and they had smiled because she did not deny that she was enjoying it. But now he could not take it at its face value, the more beautiful the face the more sceptical he was.

On the patio of the hotel – it was really an enlarged balcony over-hanging the sea – lamps were still burning among showers of pink geraniums. Somewhere the sun was coming up, turning the bay the same cosmetic pink.

'It's like Rebecca.'

'Who?'

'In the film, after she met Mr de Winter.'

'Rebecca was dead.' He felt little amusement and considerable vexation. Luise's smile, disembodied, but otherwise unlike the Cheshire Cat's, dismissed but did not release him.

He ordered tea and croissants to be brought to their room. 'It will be an early breakfast, we can have another later. Then I think we should try to get a little sleep.' He unpacked his pyjamas and threw them on the bed. He thought of sleep as an interval. Perhaps it would be the last, for afterwards nothing could remain the same, whatever he did or did not do.

He took off his jacket and went to wash his hands and face. In the mirror he saw Abby in the adjoining room. She was unpacking and as he watched her going to and fro, he heard the words, 'Not this one'.

Luise was speaking to him as she always did now, without tone or inflection or emotion, yet unquestionably it was her voice – who else's would it be inside his head?

He gripped the washbasin, he was not vengeful but he needed something solid. His life was dissolving like aspirin in a glass of water, foggy and not nearly so useful. There was a criminal element in it; he was guilty, he would be, of the crime of negligence.

'Our breakfast has come.' Abby Kennard, whom he had taken into a neglectful and, to her, possibly injurious relationship, smiled at him from the mirror. He thought what a demarcation a smile made. It put her in another world. When Luise smiled the world had been all hers.

They drank their tea and Abby ate the croissants. The Major's digestion was upset and he had no appetite. She asked did the sun shine every day, he said no, storms came suddenly and were brief and spectacular and there was a demoralising wind which could blow for days.

She had put a sort of silk bag on the pillow of the other bed. The letters A.M. were stitched in one corner. He believed it was known as a nightdress case and surely it should carry the letters P.M. as well? Then he remembered that they were her new initials: A.M. – Abby Machin.

'The sun will shine every day for us.' She went to the window and opened the shutters. They had, as the travel agent had promised, an extensive view of the bay. In the morning mist the islands floated, reminding Major Machin of the words of some poem – 'Old ships like swans asleep'. He said, 'Perhaps you'd like to go out. You must do just as you please.'

'I'll stay with you.'

He picked up the tray. 'I'll put this outside so that we're not disturbed,' and blamed himself for the interpretation she might put on that, for had he not already put it? In his own mind, in his apprehension, he had had to entertain the probability in order to retreat from it.

He removed his collar and tie and lay down on the bed with his head on his pyjamas. 'Like swans asleep' – surely *he* was not the one?

She closed the shutters and his eyelids relaxed in the gloom. He was aware of her moving about. He heard rustlings and the whisper of her skin. She lifted her arms: he felt, would swear he could feel, the air subtly change. He knew that she was standing naked beside his bed and he lay rigid, eyes closed, willing her to move away.

He awoke hours or it could have been minutes later. The room was very still and he had no incentive to open his eyes: as long as he was, or appeared to be, unconscious, nothing could be expected of him.

The idea of a middle-aged man being frightened of his bride was farcical and ironic and would provoke a few belly laughs as well. He was not frightened of Abby so much as of her capacity for being harmed. He had not wished for that sort of power over anyone, it put him to serious disadvantage, pinpointed his own inadequacy. Luise would not laugh. From her wheelchair or her bed, in pain and despair, prisoned in her all but dead flesh she had cried, 'I only want you to be happy,' and he had been unable to oblige.

He opened his eyes. Abby was at the window, she had unfastened one of the shutters and was looking out through the crack. He was relieved to see that she was fully dressed.

'Why didn't you wake me?'

'You were tired.'

'You need never feel you have to wait my convenience.' He rolled off the bed and went to the bathroom before she could say something valiant.

When he had washed and shaved and changed his shirt they went to the beach. He was surprised at the sea that was running. He supposed the wind was coming from the Cape. They were sheltered here in the lee of the rocks. The combers could be seen forming up across the bay like staves of music. When they struck the rocks their finesse was gone. They thwacked and broke, the peacock-blue water smashed into layers of blinding white that packed into the little keyhole beach. 'This is unusual at this time of year,' he said. 'I hope it's not due to the rather unpleasant wind which blows up through the Rhône Valley and drastically reduces the temperature. I fancy it is not so warm as it was.'

'Are you cold?' she said anxiously. 'You've had nothing to eat.'

He used to say, 'Are you cold? Would you like something to eat?' and Luise would say, 'Have you no conception how food disgusts me!' To Abby he said 'My wife –' and stopped. Too late. She took it as a rebuke. In God's name why? What should he rebuke her for? Blame was for him to take. If she was going to take it too, who would be innocent? 'Luise,' he said aloud.

'Did you come here with her?'

'It wouldn't have suited her. She preferred Menton. I hope it suits you here.'

'It's all new to me.'

She spoke without bravado, with only the direst uncertainty. How precarious and mistaken was her state of mind if she could believe that he would bring her to a place where he had been with Luise in order to dwell on the difference between them! On the other, or rather on the same hand, he must have given her ground for believing it.

'Rebecca,' she said, 'was clever and beautiful.'

'I shall be obliged if you will put that ridiculous idea out of your head.' She could not know that his anger was directed against himself and he was appalled at the impossibility of telling her. 'There is no comparison between a work of fiction and the present situation. Luise was a sick woman –'

'So was Rebecca, but he didn't love her.'

He walked away, facing without nostalgia Luise's undoubtedly superior intelligence, and the mockery she would have made of Abby and himself. He stood for a time seeing nothing of the staves of the sea and the incandescent sky which now had a tinge of yellow. He was making a determined effort to overlook Abby Kennard, judging that it would be better for them both. Easiness of mind could not come while she constantly exercised his thoughts in strenuous and unprofitable ways. Even a few moments to himself could lessen the tension.

The wind, suddenly getting into this keyhole in the rocks, flapped his trousers and lifted his hair. He did, for a fleeting moment, forget Abby. Where he was became a matter of colour, differing only in degree from

[187]

the tabby walls seen from his window at home. He simply existed, no strings attached, it was a pure but momentary relief. When he looked round, Abby had vanished.

He found a ledge of rock apart from the few other occupants of the beach which was private to all but hotel guests. Most of them seemed to have gone in to lunch. He perched uncomfortably on the rock and remembered Abby as he first saw her in the supermarket, her trolley enmeshed with his. She had looked no different then from the way she looked as she stood before the registrar wearing an unbecoming hat which added years to her age and made the Major feel older than he was because none but a virtual child would have worn it.

He seemed never to have got round to considering her looks. He was surprised to find that they *were* memorable: she wouldn't look much different when she was a mature woman. But he thought she might never be a mature woman.

Mercifully he had not seen her naked by his bed. It was one time she must have looked different. Had she? The mercy was that he could not picture it. He felt no charity towards himself.

A crime had been committed, another one, to dovetail with his crime against Luise. He could not atone for that but he would spend the last of his life trying to atone for the wrong he had done Abby Kennard by marrying her. He had to admit it was justice, and had reshaped his rough-hewn ends. At least his purpose was clear, he need not wonder why he was spared.

When he looked up to see her coming towards him across the beach he knew that methods would have to be found.

'I'm going for a swim.'

'I shouldn't advise it.'

She was wearing a towelling robe and her bare feet curled into the sand. 'Why not?'

'You could be dashed against the rocks.'

'I'm a strong swimmer.'

'I fear you would have little chance to swim in such a confused body of water.' He supposed she was tempted, a young person might be, by the violence which was all light and colour, nothing black or bloody or cruel, it was pure violence and a young person might want to join in. And he had told her to do as she pleased. 'I'd rather you didn't.' But that was as *he* pleased.

She didn't hear, she dropped the bathrobe and ran into the water with arms outstretched as if to embrace it. 'Shall we try?' The Major shut his eyes.

He opened them immediately. Abby was waist deep in the rioting water, arms still outstretched, to maintain her balance. Nobody else was swimming, young men watched from the rocks, a woman ran to snatch her child from a loop of foam.

The cruelty, thought Major Machin, was under the pure white water. Could there be cruelty without intent? The sea came into this cove with whatever force the wind provided, it could do minimal or monstrous harm. The degree was only in what was suffered, was all in that: so was the harm, the sea and land were geared to this sort of violence, it was a cosmic principle. No offence was intended, but people got hurt, bones were broken, flesh torn, ships and lungs burst asunder. And Abby had put herself into the workings. Hadn't she said she loved the sea and would rather die that way than any other?

He glimpsed her head, then lost sight of it under the layering foam. A wall of water hung across the whole of the bay and reflected in it the yellowing sky. The wave, before it broke, was the colour of brass. It piled in, pounding the sand with a force which the Major felt through the soles of his feet.

When it receded it threatened to suck out the keyhole beach and the hotel above it. A figure was left grovelling in the foam. The Major thanked God and swallowed – his heart had been in his throat.

Abby stood up. Below those chapped cheeks of hers she was white-skinned and slightly tawny from the light off the sea. She staggered, fell to her knees and struggled up again. She seemed dazed, as well she might be. Something else was wrong – amiss.

She wore only half her costume. The sea had undressed her, torn off and carried away the top of her bikini. The same cosmic principle had tossed her up on the beach and would take her back with the under-tow. She seemed unaware of her loss, or if she was aware, she judged it more important to keep on her feet than cover her breasts. The young men watching from the rock applauded and shouted joyous encouragement.

Major Machin ran, pitching in the soft sand, and pulled off his jacket as he went. He reached her, mindful but not minding as the water surged round his ankles.

She stood in the ebb, shining like a new penny. Her cheeks were not chapped, they were red and warm. She smelt of youth and strength and the cleanliness of the sea. The Major put his coat about her, and his arms.